PAY DIRT

Adventure, Adversity & Betrayal

in Frontier Alaska

by
Otis Hahn and Alice Vollmar

About the Authors

Otis Hahn was born in Black Duck, Minnesota, in 1927, attended school in Mizpah, Minnesota, for eight years, and grew up in the timber country of northern Minnesota among the rivers and lakes. Severely dyslexic, Hahn found the wilderness around him a more effective teacher than books, and he spent his youth hunting, fishing, and trapping.

Photo by Natures Photography

In 1950, Hahn spent the first of many summers in Alaska, where he met his wife, Audrey. During the early fifties, he worked seasonally in a Livengood gold mine and for the Alaska Road Commission. The couple returned to farming for the next twenty-five years in Minnesota, where they raised two sons and two daughters. Today they have six grandchildren.

Hahn always dreamed of going back to Alaska and looking for gold, and he finally did so in 1981. "It was an adventure I'll never forget," he says.

"I've got a story to tell about mining gold in Alaska," Otis Hahn told writer Alice Vollmar a few years ago. "If you're interested, let's get together and talk about it."

Their meeting led to a collaboration between Hahn and Vollmar to write *Pay Dirt*. Based in Minneapolis, Vollmar is a regionally noted travel writer whose freelance credits include a travel guidebook, *Minnesota Wisconsin Travel-Smart Trip Planner*, and articles in *Travel & Leisure* as well as numerous other magazines. She is married and the mother of six children.

Photo by Liza Foume´

As a former tutor, Vollmar was sensitive to Otis Hahn's struggle with dyslexia. Through tape recordings and interviews with Hahn, Vollmar was pleased to help him share his Alaska adventure.

PAY DIRT

First Printing, 1998
Revised Second Printing, 2000

Author - Otis Hahn & Alice Vollmar
Publisher - McCleery & Sons Publishing
Cover Design and Map Illustration - Robert Washnieski

International Standard Book Number: 0-9700624-4-3
Printed in the United States of America.

To order additional copies of
PAY DIRT
($15.95 + $3.50 shipping & handling each)

SEND CHECK OR MONEY ORDER ALONG WITH MAILING ADDRESS TO:
McCLEERY & SONS PUBLISHING
PO Box 248, Gwinner, ND 58040-0248

OR ORDER BY PHONE WITH CREDIT CARD 1-888-568-6329

OR ORDER ONLINE WITH CREDIT CARD at www.jmcompanies.com

Orders by check allow longer delivery time.
Money order and credit card orders will be shipped within 48 hours.
Payable in US funds. No cash accepted.

This offer is subject to change without notice.

Contents

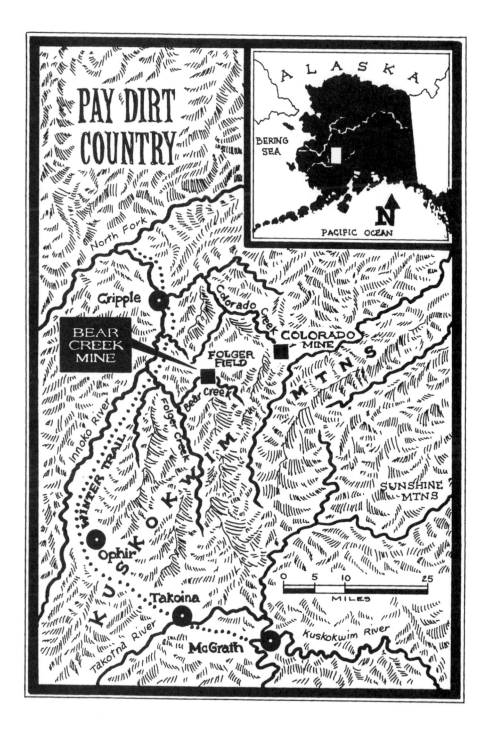

Author's Note

We were out camping in the North Woods in Minnesota a few years back, me and my kids and grandkids. We got a campfire going and put young Heather to bed in her tent. The rest of us sat around, watching the fire, listening to the flames crackle and hiss, and I got to talking about Alaska. A couple of hours later, the talk kind of died down. All of a sudden, Heather piped up from the tent, "More stories, Grandpa Otis. Tell more stories about Alaska, Grandpa. Please."

CHAPTER 1

North to Alaska

The pilot was a talker, jabbering nonstop since we left Anchorage. "You can only get through the Alaska Range in three places between Anchorage and the town of McGrath," he said as jagged peaks—a wall of white-topped mountains—rose in front of our airplane.

We headed straight for the tallest one. The rocky clefts and mountain ledges grew more and more distinct, and my fingernails dug ditches in my palms.

"Hey, Otis, you want to try your luck and pick the pass?" asked the pilot and grinned.

"Not today," I said.

"Come to think of it, you do look a little unsteady." Another toothy grin. "Well, my first time through here was nearly my last, and I almost lost it flying in a week ago."

The plane dropped suddenly and my stomach lurched. I braced myself for the worst. Seconds before we smashed head-on into the rocky wall, the mountain opened up and let us through. And suddenly we were descending into McGrath.

People stood beside the asphalt runway, watching the plane taxi to a stop—a blur of nut-brown beardless Native faces, black braids, a few blond heads and shaggy brown beards, and one stocky, brown-mustached guy in jeans and a red shirt. He stepped out from the crowd and extended his hand.

"I'm Hank," he said. I grabbed my gear and followed him.

Hank was old Jim Hunter's son-in-law. It was Hank's phone call that got me to McGrath: "I hear you're interested in buying a placer gold mine in Alaska," he'd said. "My family's got one for sale."

That was three days ago. Jim Hunter had been mining in the Bush for twenty-eight years; his family thought it was time for him to sell. I tossed my duffle into the Cessna 180 Hank had waiting and climbed in.

On September 25, 1981, Hank and I were on our way to the mine, fifty air-miles from McGrath, off the Kuskokwim River on Bear Creek. The only way in and out was by air.

Thirty-five minutes later, the plane bumped along on a short runway skirted by dark-green scrub spruce, aspen, and willow. Mountains on every side shut out the world. A dirt road led into the trees to the mine camp. We shouldered our bags and set off.

Hank filled me in on Jim.

"He's a tough old fellow, Otis," he told me. "He's had three Athabascan Indian wives and lost two sons to Bush airplane accidents out here. There've been plenty of people interested in buying the mine over the years, but the old guy hasn't been in the frame of mind to sell before."

We walked down into the cut at the spot where the mine had first started. In the cut—land prepared for sluicing—two beat-up crawler tractors sat mired in mud. The dragline looked in sorry shape, and tools and discarded parts were scattered everywhere.

The camp amounted to a handful of battered buildings—

a green-roofed, tin-sided cookhouse on skids, a bunkhouse and a few sheds, a meat cache, and a small log cabin. A black mongrel dog, minus one leg, loped toward us, barking.

Hank opened the door to the cookhouse. My eyes took a minute to adjust to the dim light. The long, narrow room was jammed with so much stuff that I didn't see Jim right away.

"You're here when you said you'd be," I heard from the back of the room. Jim was sitting at a long table, beyond a couple dozen liquor bottles and stacks of pots and pans and plates.

"I'm a man of my word," I said, walking over to the table.

Sun and wind had leathered his face, and he hadn't shaved for a couple of days. Jim looked me up and down. "A man of his word," he muttered. "Well, Otis, that's the kind of man I want to deal with."

He grabbed a bottle off the table, poured some whiskey into a dented tin cup, and slid it across the table toward me. He splashed whiskey into a cup for himself and tossed it down.

"You'd have a tough time out here," he said, wiping his toothless mouth with the back of his hand. "A damn tough time. The mine's remote and getting fuel and parts in costs a lot, even if you've already got your own airplane. You do have an airplane?"

I took a swig from my cup and felt the liquid burn all the way down. Jim was watching me through squinted eyes. "Well, no," I answered, "I don't own a plane, and I'm not a pilot."

The man cackled, poured more whiskey into his cup, and downed it. "Hell, you're gonna be doing a lot a walking then, fella-from-Minnesota. It's at least two hours to the Strants on foot. They're your closest neighbors, young David and his dad, miners over on Colorado Creek."

Jim spent the rest of the night tipping the bottle and talking. I listened: He'd been raised in Kansas, rode the rails when he was sixteen, and made it up to Alaska more than fifty years ago. He'd been around Fairbanks and out on Bear Creek ever since.

I spread my sleeping bag in the cookhouse bedroom that night and wondered what I was letting myself in for. Was there gold in Jim's mine? Would the weather let me get out for a good look at the mine? It was decent today, but being late September, that could change fast.

I knew that from years back when I'd lived in the Fairbanks area. In fact, I recognized a lot of the names old Jim'd brought up in his talking. Trapper John, for one. The spring of 1951, Audrey and I honeymooned driving up the Alcan Highway. I'd managed to get a job with the Alaska Road Commission, and they gave me a road grader and a pickup truck, and put me in charge of maintaining the Livengood Road. That's when I met Trapper John. He took me out to see his prize timber wolf pelt. It measured nine and a half feet long.

"Alaska grows 'em that size," he said, stroking his beard.

I came to believe the unbelievable in this territory the United States bought from Russia in 1867. Admitted as a state in 1959, Alaska dwarfs Texas and covers 570,373 square miles. It's a place that shatters expectations. Alaska is wild and rough and like no place else.

Luck was with me on my first trip to the Northland. I was twenty-three. My brother Ray and I drove the Alcan Highway, determined to get to Alaska and land jobs—that was before I married sweet Audrey. It was cold, dipping to forty-two below zero that February. Along the way, we rescued a family whose car had quit. And green as we were, Ray and I found work in a lead mine.

After I married Audrey, we spent four summers in a road commission camp alongside a river that gave us all the fish we could eat. That was living in the wilderness, all right.

A fellow got lost in the Bush that first summer. There was a full-scale hunt going on for fourteen days before the officials gave up the search. Some days later, I was working on the road and spied something way off in a flat. I picked up my field glasses—the "something" was a man! I got down off my machine pronto, crossed the river, and worked my way to an open spot. About a quarter of a mile from the figure, I yelled, "Hello there!"

The man dropped from sight. I kept working my way to him, but I kept low. The guy might be half crazy by now. Did he have a rifle and shells? That worried me. I didn't want to be shot at. Then I could see him—a hump hiding under a mat of moss. I inched myself up close, reached in, and yanked the guy out. His shoes were gone, his feet were swollen, and he smelled something awful. His hands clutched at his chest, and he looked at me with dark eyes gone vacant and wild. He had a piece of fur under his arm— a dead and rotting rabbit, which accounted for the smell. He'd probably been eating on it for days.

I walked and dragged the guy to my pickup and got him into camp. But he wouldn't budge, just cowered on the seat. So I drove to Fairbanks to the police station. On the drive I talked a bit and said, "You must have had a bad time of it. My name's Otis. What's yours?" He started to look around more normal-like but he didn't speak.

"Never thought we'd see this guy alive," the policeman on duty said. "Never!" I left the fellow at the station. I've often wondered what became of him—and how on earth he'd stayed alive.

The Bush is no place to be lost in. My experiences in Alaska taught me a lot. After four summers in the road camp, Audrey and I took over Dad's farm in northern Minnesota, near Mizpah. We raised four kids there, grew grain, and had hogs and cattle. Then, although we still lived on the place, we handed the farm over to our youngest son, Dave. That's when I started thinking about Alaska again.

Back when I worked the Livengood Road, men would come out of the Bush and talk about gold mining. I'd always wanted to try my hand at mining some of that Alaska gold. So, I decided to try to find myself a gold mine.

Of course, I had plenty of doubts about this Bear Creek mine—and a few about myself. Was I up to living in the Bush at fifty-four? Could I get the mine into working shape? Sure, I was toughened up from years of operating heavy equipment and farming, but still. . . . Then there was the big question: Was there any gold in this mine?

The old cookhouse creaked and sighed. I listened to the wind rattle the windows, and finally, I fell asleep.

CHAPTER 2

Coming to Terms

"Breakfast," Jim said at my door before daylight the next morning. I could smell strong coffee brewing. Old Jim had flapjacks on the stove and potatoes frying in a pan. Hank was up, too.

We ate, and Jim gave Hank instructions: "You take Otis out and spend all day with him. You watch him pan, show him the places to pan, and the whole spread I've got here."

That's what we did—spent the whole day down on our knees, panning. I found gold in every pan that I took. Fine gold and some really good flakes. By the middle of the afternoon, my adrenaline was rushing.

The amount of ground Jim had was generous—more than seven miles on Bear and Graham Creeks, plus five claims over on Cripple Creek, which had a good reputation. Cripple was very popular in the days before and just after World War II. That creek has yielded up a lot of money.

However, there wasn't much hope of using old Jim's equipment. The only positive on that count was a good stock of pipe and a lot of giants for spraying the mud and overburden off the gravel. Giants are oversized nozzles that create the water pressure you need to get to the best pay, usually about a foot above the bedrock. The pipe and giants were usable, a plus because that kind of equipment would be hard to fly in on a small plane.

Alaska is the land of the small airplane. All those years ago, a small plane flew Ray and me from Fairbanks to jobs with Callahan Lead and Zinc. We were happy to leave the Fairbanks tent camp—three bunks and one lightbulb per tent for fifty dollars a week. All the tent-dwellers were looking for work. Ray and I considered ourselves lucky to be getting that airplane ride. We'd made it to Alaska—and had jobs.

When Hank and I came in that night, Jim started needling me: "I thought maybe a feller from Minnesota might need lessons on how to pan. I was a little worried about you out there, Otis."

I shrugged and said simply, "Jim, I knew you were right here to show me how if I got in over my head."

If he hoped to get a rise out of me, it wasn't going to work. I just let him rattle on. Hank set about fixing us supper, and I went outside to take a good look at the camp. It wasn't scenic: old oil drums and debris were scattered everywhere. But I was glad to see the oil drums. Alaska's state flower, that's what those fifty-five-gallon steel drums have been called. You see them abandoned along roads and wherever machinery runs. Up here, when you need a water tank, culverts, a rain barrel, a bathtub, maybe even a sauna, those steel drums blossom into hundreds of uses.

Then I noticed the good-sized pool behind the cookhouse. A few steps closer, the pool turned out to be teeming with Arctic grayling. That sent me back inside in search of fishing line and hooks. Jim found some old fishing gear of his, and I pulled in grayling after grayling. I brought a full pail of fish into the cookhouse.

Old Jim stood there, shaking his head. "One thing about a Minnesota miner out here," he said. "If you can't make money mining, you can always catch fish. At least you won't starve."

That night, I did some serious contemplating. I'd come up here with a commitment from fourteen men, mostly professional people from Minnesota who had money to invest and were itching to back a gold-mining venture. We'd talked at length about setting up a corporation; each person agreed to contribute twenty-five thousand dollars to get started, myself included. And I'd signed a promissory note at the bank for my share of the start-up investment. I wondered if Jim would actually sell. And if he did, what would be his terms?

In the morning, an airplane landed on the camp airstrip.

"That's the Strants' plane," Jim said, "David probably wants to get a look at you."

I wanted a look at him, too. David stood quite a few inches taller than my five feet, eight inches. He had close-cropped brown hair receding at the forehead and a friendly smile. He'd brought along his top hand, Craig Allen, a heavy equipment operator with a bushy black beard, blue stocking cap, and two-hundred-plus pounds on his six-foot-plus frame.

Craig's first words were, "What's happening on the Outside?" He and his wife, Fran, had been in the Bush about three years and had a couple of little kids. To my way of thinking, Craig, who was also a trapper, fit my idea of a true mountain man, beard and all.

David was straightforward about his mining operation on Colorado Creek. We talked the whole morning, me envisioning having him as a neighbor. It seemed okay.

"The pay at Bear Creek is fine gold, just as we have over on Colorado Creek," he said when I walked him back to his plane. "My dad was a partner with Jim at one time, but they had too many disagreements and dissolved the partnership. As far as the creek is concerned, it's as good a creek as there is around. But you will have a problem getting machinery in here."

I eyed his airplane.

"Would you be interested in flying for me?" I asked straight out.

His reply was just as straight: "No. I don't do custom flying. Ace Airway in McGrath needs the business. I'd advise you to hire them."

Before he left, David said he'd help me out any way except flying if I bought the mine.

Time was getting short. Ace Airway was due to pick me up in a few hours. I looked over the operation one more time and went inside.

I told Jim I was interested in the mine. He nodded. I asked what he'd want for it.

"My terms are simple," Jim said. He rubbed his chin stubble, looking hard at me. "I want seventy thousand dollars for my camp and everything you see here. You give me ten thousand down and ten thousand a year for the next six years. There'll be no interest to it. But I want 20 percent royalty—20 percent of the gold you take out of the sluice box."

"That's a steep royalty, Jim," I told him. Then I went out for a hike to mull things over. I wasn't crazy about Jim's 20 percent, but the investors would be happy to get into mining for ten thousand dollars a year. We'd be paying no interest on the balance. I thought the money end of it had a chance to work out.

"You've got yourself a deal," I said when I returned. Hank got out some paper and a pen, sat down at the cookhouse table, and wrote up the agreement. He read it aloud to Jim and me. I had him add that Jim'd have to be present at cleanups to make sure he got his share out of the box. That suited Jim, too.

When the plane came to pick me up, the three of us flew into town and went to an attorney's office to have the contract drawn up. I filled him in on my arrangements and told him my investors were forming a corporation back in International Falls, Minnesota.

From the attorney's office, I called an investor in

International Falls, my liaison with the larger group, to give him the news. Well, they'd been meaning to have things pulled together by now, he told me, but they didn't have the money there yet.

Listening to the conversation, Jim started to squirm in his chair. Finally, he said, "Otis, if you don't have the money to buy a mine with, what the hell are you doing up here?"

I told my contact I'd call him back and hung up, none too happy myself.

"It'll all be straightened out, Jim," I said. "Everything is fine; it just takes some arranging to move quickly and handle everything by phone."

Jim stood up and started for the door. "Okay, Otis, but this sure is enough talkin' for today. Let's get out of here." The attorney set 10 A.M. the next morning as the time we'd meet to sign the final papers. Hank was headed for the airport to catch a plane back to his home in the Aleutian Islands, so we said good-bye. Jim headed out the door on his heels.

Before I left the office, the attorney said, "You've had a bit of luck, Otis. Lots of people have tried to buy the Bear Creek claim, but Jim Hunter either wouldn't even talk to them or said he'd sell and then backed out. This looks like it has a chance of working out."

After supper in McGrath, I called my International Falls contact from a phone booth.

"What's going on? I thought the investors had already pooled their outlay in our International Falls bank account," I said. I told him that deals go fast here, with no hemming or hawing. He said he hadn't realized the speed of doing business in Alaska. He told me to give him an hour and call back.

I did. "Go ahead and sign the papers, Otis," he said. He'd called other investors and told me a check for $10,000 would be in the mail.

Jim had a house in McGrath, and he'd suggested that I sleep there. The town lies on a big bend of the Kuskokwim River. In the simple one-story frame houses sprawling every which way lived the 350-some residents, 75 percent of them Native Alaskans, Athabascan Indians. A considerable part of the town's space went to the residents' dogs—about 250 of them.

I walked the town and counted two saloons, a boarding house, hardware store, cafe, grocery, and two bush airplane services. The main attraction in town was the mile-long asphalt runway with its control tower, the site of comings and goings.

The oldest part of town was where a U.S. Commissioner named Peter McGrath started a trading post and recording office back in 1907. That's where Jim's directions led; I found his house and bedded down on the old couch.

Dogs, hundreds of dogs barking in unison, woke me up in the night. The chorus howled away and then, suddenly, stopped—as if on cue from the wolf blood mingled in the bunch. The dogs got me to remembering how the constant gabble of geese aroused my curiosity when Ray and I worked for Callahan. You're hearing the geese at Yukon Flats, I was told; that's where geese go to spend the summer. I hired a kid with a Piper Cub to fly me over the flats. Geese and goslings were everywhere, along with moose and their newborn calves. It was a wildlife utopia, a nursery in the wild.

Jim didn't show up at his house all that night; I walked into the attorney's office at 10 A.M., and the waiting room was empty. No sign of Jim anywhere. I paced, looked out the windows at the buildings squatted along McGrath's streets, and waited ten, fifteen minutes. Then I told the attorney I was going out looking for him.

I headed for the saloon that's situated handy to the end of the runway. A couple of airplanes sat right outside the saloon door. My hunch was on target. The old guy was there all right, at the far end of the long room talking to two men with polished boots and solid gold belt buckles. I took a stool at the other end of the bar and ordered a beer.

In a couple of minutes, Jim shuffled over to me. "Well,

you know, Otis, I've changed my mind. These guys flew in to offer me more money, and I'm going to sell to them."

I took a slow sip off my beer, then took a second sip before I swiveled my bar stool around and looked him straight in the eyes.

"Jim Hunter, all you have to do is reimburse me for an airplane ticket back to Minnesota," I said. "I agreed to come up to Alaska and talk with you on the twenty-fifth—and I did. I carried out my end of the arrangement, and I was on time. When we flew into McGrath yesterday, I thought we had a deal."

Jim's eyes were rheumy from the liquor that must have helped the other deal along. I continued, "Look, when I was in Alaska thirty years ago, the old-timers kept their word. But I can see that's all changed now."

I watched Jim's face turn red. His arm shot out and he grabbed my shoulder, his fingers tightening in a vise grip.

"My word's always been good, Otis," he said.

He turned around to face the other two guys who'd moved up closer to listen to our exchange. "This is the guy who's getting the creek."

I hustled Jim out of there and up to the attorney's office. He signed the papers, and so did I.

Evidently, the Bush grapevine'd been buzzing about what was going on at old Jim's mine. Someone who'd once tried to buy the mine and been turned down had sent the two fellows up from Fairbanks to persuade Jim. They came close to succeeding.

The old miner headed back to the bar after the signing. I knew I had just a few weeks to get the mine ready for winter. His old crawler tractors had to be taken out of the mud and put on high ground. And the dragline needed to be taken out of the cut. In winter, glaciers build up in the cuts due to water seeping through the sand and gravel. It freezes and builds up, causing the glacier to rise. Left where it was, the dragline would be history come spring.

So I had to get moving fast. I called Minnesota and arranged for a couple of young men to come up. One was a boy, Tim Worker, who'd worked for me cutting timber in the woods. We'd talked about mining, and I wanted him to have a chance to work in the mine. The other was Brent Delaney, an investor's friend who'd agreed to come up and help. They said they'd fly into Bear Creek the next week.

Then I headed for the saloon to pack Jim into an Ace Airway plane and fly back to the mine. He was in bad shape, but the pilot and I got him aboard.

It hit me—the full impact of what I'd done—in midair.

"I'll be damned," I said aloud to the incoherent Jim. He groaned.

"I'll be damned," I said again. I grinned. "You got yourself a gold mine, Otis Hahn. Wahoo!"

Jim's chin sank down on his chest, and he started to snore.

CHAPTER 3

First Days as a Miner

It was late afternoon by the time we got to Bear Creek, and the pilot was in a hurry to leave while he had daylight. He helped me lift Jim out of the airplane and took off to fly the fifty air-miles (113 by ground) to McGrath.

I struggled to get Jim up on his rubbery legs. A raw wind whistled through the trees, carrying a wintry bite. We staggered toward camp. Jim's three-legged mutt bounded out to greet us and kept circling our legs, slowing us down.

"What on earth am I doing out in the middle of nowhere with a half-dead miner and a three-legged dog?" I asked myself. It sounded like a bad joke.

I looked at my sorry companions and couldn't help but laugh. It wasn't the first time I'd ended up in a ridiculous situation, or the last.

I finally got Jim into camp and to bed. Feeling about as alone as a person can, I heated up a can of stew, listened to the wind trying to tear the cookhouse apart, and crawled into my sleeping bag.

The smell of coffee woke me. Jim was up cooking

potatoes and pancakes in the kitchen as usual. While we ate, he made a proposal to me.

"I've got a little cut that you and I could sluice," he said. "We just need to get the pipes in. The drain would have to be dug to get rid of the water above, but I think there's maybe thirty thousand dollars we could get fairly quick. I've been trying all summer but I couldn't get anyone to help. What do you think, Otis?"

Old Jim's recovery amazed me. And I liked the idea of getting a little ground through the sluice box and seeing what we really had. I nodded. "Sure, let's give it a try."

On with the gum boots and down into the cut we went. "Quick" turned out to be five days of problems. We got the old dragline started, but the tracks wouldn't stay on it. We fought it, got ourselves caked with mud, and only managed to get some of the muck out of the drain. But it gave me a sample of what we'd be up against in the spring. I knew I'd darn well better handpick a hard-working crew.

We were down in the cut one afternoon when the Ace Airway plane flew over. Tim and Brent were coming in. I headed for the airstrip but it took me a good half hour to get there. The airplane took off, and pretty soon I heard voices. The one I knew was Tim's said, "I'm sure if Otis said this is the place we're supposed to be, then this must be right."

I stepped off the trail and stayed quiet. They walked right by—Tim, compact, every inch muscle, with a shock of red hair and Brent, taller than Tim, sandy-haired and lean—both barely in their twenties, wearing new jeans and looking like a pair of lost kids.

"Where do you guys think you're going?" I yelled. They whirled around and broke into grins. We talked steadily on the way to camp. Then they set to cleaning the bunkhouse enough so they'd have a place to sleep. After supper, we sat around listening to Jim's mining tales. Out of the blue, Tim asked, "Say, Jim, are you a Christian believer?" That brought Jim up short.

"Me?" he said. "A Christian believer? Tim, I don't believe in nothing I can't see."

That set off some lengthy conversation related to what God is and isn't. Tim is a Seventh-Day Adventist, and he and Jim sure didn't see eye to eye. Pretty soon, Brent chimed in. I sat back and enjoyed the show. Then Tim told me, "I don't work on Saturdays because of my religion." He meant it. I lost a worker for one day each week, including later on when we worked fourteen-hour days, seven days a week to get things going.

On the first morning of Tim and Brent's arrival, Jim cooked up a big spread. We each grabbed a spot at the long table, surrounded by half of the kitchen utensils plus Jim's whiskey bottles—full ones and empties he used for pitchers and storing liquids.

"Here's the pancakes, boys," Jim said, setting down a platter of golden brown cakes. Tim took a plate, piled it high, pulled the top off a bottle, and poured. Whiskey flooded his plate.

"Hey! Watch it, young feller!" Jim sputtered. "If you want whiskey, at least put it in a cup. That stuff is too expensive out here to waste on pancakes. And here I thought you were a teetotaling preacher fellow."

Tim chose his syrup carefully after that.

At the mine, we cleared the drain in Jim's little cut as best we could. The weather turned nasty—half snow, half rain. We finished cleaning out the bunkhouse and put things into partial order. Tim and Brent picked up the scattered tools; we got the crawlers out of the mud and put things into the sheds.

Eventually, we had to abandon the little cut. We didn't have time left to set up pumps and sluice, not when the ground was already stiff in the mornings. Jim was disappointed, but I didn't want my equipment frozen in the mud. You couldn't help feeling a little bit for Jim Hunter—it was hard for him to let go of the operation.

We got ready to fly back to the Lower 48. Jim wanted to know our plans for the spring. "I can't tell you what to do," he'd say, "but I can tell you what not to do." Then he'd elaborate. He hung around that last day while we closed up the sheds, talking, trying, I think, to scare us off—seeing this as his last chance. We heard about all the miners he'd seen come out into the Bush and fail. He dredged up bear stories, too, and tales about men who got hurt out here with no way to get help.

I do know about bears. We lost Audrey's dog Blondie to an old grizzly one summer at the Livengood road camp. Tore the door off our meat cache and took the moose meat, too. I found the grizzly and shot him, out of fear that he'd come back. Once a bear comes into camp, you know you're in for trouble. I don't much care to shoot them, but at times a person's got no choice. A bear that comes into camp is not something to take lightly.

As I double-propped sagging doors and lubricated machinery, a part of me listened seriously to what old Jim was saying. Come spring, we'd be out here on our own.

The Ace Airway plane came that afternoon. I shook hands with Jim before we boarded the plane and even patted his old mutt's head.

"You'll have your work cut out for you next year," Jim said. "Hope it don't kill you, Otis."

CHAPTER 4

Cat on Ice

The little yellow house on the farm at Mizpah looked like a palace after the weeks at the Bear Creek mine. I could smell bread baking when I opened the door. Audrey's crusty fried chicken and mashed potatoes with homegrown squash and string beans never tasted better.

"How'd you like to be a gold mine cook?" I asked her.

She smiled and answered, "Well, it sure is too lonely around here without you, Otis."

I knew that'd solve two problems in the best possible way. We'd eat well come next mining season, and Audrey and I'd be together. It felt good to get home, but there was little time for resting up. Immediately, I got to work on hiring my mining crew and rounding up equipment.

For a start-up crew, I hired Tim and Brent, plus a couple of other fellows used to the outdoors, and one that wasn't—a distant cousin's boy, Andy Davis, a blond fellow with a groomed beard, in his thirties, married several times but never really settled down. Andy was a mechanic, and we'd need one. He'd also be able to help out with reading, bookwork, and letter-writing—which was vitally important to me. Because of my lifelong struggle with severe dyslexia,

I've always had to rely on Audrey or other people to help with any paperwork.

Andy was itching to be part of my crew.

"It's going to be darn tough, and the mine's out in the wilderness," I told him.

"I want to come along," he said.

The biggest chore ahead of me was finding a Caterpillar tractor and a rubber-tired loader to work the mine. Then, how would I get the machines out to Bear Creek? That kept me awake nights. An airplane big enough to transport even a partially dismantled Caterpillar could land at McGrath, but definitely not on our Bush country airstrips.

"I know! I'll put that Cat on ice, that's what I'll do," I told Audrey one night. "We'll drive the Cat out to the mine from McGrath. I think that'll work if we cross the Kuskokwim River before spring thaws the ice."

Money for the Cat and loader would come from the funds pooled by the investors when we met in October. Right after my return from Bear Creek, we'd had a meeting in International Falls. I figured the tractor would cost around $100,000 and the loader from $60,000 to $80,000. Each of the fourteen investors and myself kicked in $25,000 to get started. At that meeting, I was elected president of the corporation, which we called White Wolf Mining. We also elected a chairman and treasurer.

It was agreed that I'd receive minutes of their monthly meetings, report the mining progress, and bill the corporation for expenses. The chairman and treasurer would oversee the funds and pay the bills for expenses from a White Wolf Mining business account. I'd also deposit checks from the sale of gold to that account.

"I think we've got a good mine, and I'll do my best to get it operating and to get the gold out," I told them. Everybody left the meeting in good spirits.

I found a fellow on the West Coast with a Cat and loader for sale. The machines were already up in Alaska, so Andy and I flew there to look at them. The seller was reputable, and the equipment came with a year's guarantee—the machines were exactly what I'd hoped to find. So I bought them.

It took three air trips to get the disassembled Cat and loader flown from Anchorage to McGrath. Towering mounds of snow banked the McGrath runway. When the C-130 Hercules plane set down with the first load, the smell of diesel fuel mingled with hot rubber from the plane's tires. The pilot opened a window and hollered down, "Are you Mr. Hahn?"

"Yes. Do you have my tractor parts?" I yelled back.

"Sure do—about thirty tons of them," he grinned.

The pilot opened the big back door; inside, the equipment was on steel skids. I'd hired a loader to pull the skids out of the plane. When we hooked up to the loader, the skids screeched and groaned coming off the plane onto the runway, and a fierce wind whipped at us. The air service gave us twenty-four hours to assemble the Cat and get it off the runway.

I'd talked to fellows in the town who said they'd hire on to help assemble the Cat. When the last equipment load came in, I went to the bar and said I was ready to start working on my Cat. Not a one of those guys came out to work. It was thirty-five below zero with a thirty-mile-per-hour wind the morning that Andy and I started putting the thing together outside by ourselves, every breath a white cloud, our teeth chattering. Our fingers were so numb that wrenches slipped out of our hands. I'd been cold in Minnesota, but nothing like this.

An old yellow pickup pulled up beside us, windows frosted over except for one peephole. A big husky guy with a gray beard got out. "I'm Dan Heron," he said. "You fellows got a hell of a job on a nice day like this. You'll need some blocks for the front of the Cat, and I've got some in the back of the truck. And a gas heater, too. I'll start it 'cause you're going to need to keep your hands warm. And I'll just leave my old pickup here. If you need something, you can't be walking all day."

We thanked the guy. Before he left he told us to come to his house to eat. "My wife's cooking salmon belly stew for supper, and you're invited," he said.

"That sounds mighty good," I told him. We got the Cat put together by 9:30 P.M. and headed to Dan's house for some of that stew. He loaned us a canvas and a motor heater to warm up the Cat overnight. Next morning, we drove the tractor off the runway and found a place to park it until next spring.

Then we flew back to Minnesota, and I bought a tandem truck for $5,400. On February 23, I loaded up the big pumps and power units and other equipment, and Andy and I headed for Alaska on the Alcan Highway. It took five days of jouncing over snow-crusted roads to get to Anchorage, and I left the truck running all night in the Yukon to keep it from freezing up—a common practice up there. We arranged to have the equipment flown to McGrath and sold the truck for fourteen thousand dollars in Anchorage.

On March 1, in McGrath, I sent a Bush radio message to Craig Allen out on Colorado Creek. He'd agreed to drive the Cat and loader out to the mine along with Andy. I told him the equipment was ready to move. He radioed back that he'd be coming in.

The next day, in the frigid, gray early morning light, Andy and I walked a snow-walled path down to the river and cut a hole with a power saw about twenty feet from the bank. The ice measured thirty-six inches; I knew we needed at least thirty inches to support the fifty-ton Cat. Next, we coaxed the cold Cat into starting, its engine noise shattering the frigid air. Then I had Andy back the Cat over the hole. The water didn't rise a bit. "Go ahead, Andy. Drive it across," I said.

I watched, holding my breath. The yellow Cat crawled across the river ice—and made it to the other side. Andy let out a war whoop, and I hollered back. Then he hiked back to join me, and we headed to the Iditarod Cafe for hot coffee and breakfast.

"When you gonna take the Cat across the river?" asked one of the old sourdoughs in the cafe. "We got some money bet on whether or not you're gonna make it."

"Well, the fellows betting against us are going to lose some money," I grinned, blowing on my cold fingers. "The Cat's sitting across the river right now."

Andy and I'd rented a cabin in town, and Craig came knocking at the door the next day. I told him I wanted them to get off right away.

"Sorry, Otis, but we can't. The Iditarod Trail Sled Dog Race is coming through, so we'll have to wait until the last team passes by."

For six long days, we watched lean running dogs breathing white steam clouds and heard the jingle of harness metal as sleds hissed along the trail. People clustered beside the trail, bundled up against the cold, to see the dog teams. McGrath is one of the dozen or so Bush villages on the trail that follows the old dog team mail route from Knik to Nome, dating back to 1910. A musher named Joe Redington Sr. and a historian, Dorothy Page, get credit for launching the sled dog race in 1967. It's grown into a major sporting event. Since our intended route ran along part of the trail, Craig, a musher himself, just plain refused to budge until the dogs had passed through.

Meanwhile, I worried about the ice thinning out. To pass time, I stopped in to visit old Jim Hunter. He was fuming.

"See this, Otis?" he said, holding up a half-full bottle.

"Looks like a bottle of whiskey to me," I said.

"Well, Otis, it sure ain't whiskey. I got this friend who I told could stay here, see. He comes for the races every year. Well, he drank up my whiskey, then pissed in the bottle. And just left it sitting here like it was full. What would you do about a friend like that?"

"I think I'd cork it up and save it for him next year," I said. "And I'd offer him the first swig."

The sky hung low with clouds on the morning I watched my Cat and loader head away from McGrath. My plan was to hire a plane to fly over as often as possible each day, so I could get help to Craig and Andy if it was needed. We figured it'd be a four-day drive, if there weren't any problems.

Three hours later, Andy tramped into my cabin in McGrath. "Looks like we're in bad trouble," he said. "Craig took a shortcut through a slough and the big dozer fell in. The whole back end is under water."

I went out with Andy, and what I saw gave my insides a turn. The dozer blade and front end of the tracks protruded from an ice-rimmed hole. When I tried to push a pole down behind the track, it went down eight feet. There was no way to put anything under or behind the Cat to help it climb out. But maybe, I thought, we could get a big tractor to pull the Cat out.

Back in town, we found a fellow with a D-7 Caterpillar that had a winch on it. But the guy was hesitant to come out on the ice. "I'll let you know in the morning," he said. Andy and I shoveled snow over the tracks on the Caterpillar to keep the tractor from freezing in. I had a lot riding on the outcome. It was a long night for me.

In the morning, David Strant flew in and gave us a lift out to the almost-submerged Cat. He shook his head and said, "So, you own a gold mine, Otis." That stuck in my head. I knew we had lots to learn. Lesson number one was: Be very careful where you try to go with a fifty-ton Cat!

Then I saw the D-7 tractor coming up behind us. We hooked the winch up to my Cat. The D-7 pulled it out—and my Cat broke through the ice again. That happened over and over. The cold turned Craig's beard a frosty white, but underneath my hooded parka, my shirt was soaked with sweat. Then, the D-7 gave a pull, wrenched the Cat out, and out it stayed. The Cat had reached a spot with enough moss and timber under the ice to hold it up. I suddenly felt weak in the knees.

"After this, no shortcuts through sloughs," I told Craig. He wholeheartedly agreed. I also told him to check the ice with an auger before trying to cross any rivers and to push timber and snow out on the ice before they crossed. That way there'd be something underneath the Cat's tracks if the ice did give way. "I'll fly out first thing in the morning to check on you," I told them.

Before David dropped me off in McGrath, he said, "I want you to see something, Otis." We passed over a different slough. I looked down where he pointed and saw, barely visible, the exhaust pipes of a Cat. David told me that Cat had broken through the ice three years ago, sank, and stayed.

I didn't fly out to check on my crew the next morning. In fact, I couldn't fly out of McGrath for three days. A snowstorm dumped snow steadily, and no Ace Airway planes were allowed to fly. Boy, did it rankle me that I couldn't pilot my own small plane!

In pure desperation, on day four, I found a risk-taking bush pilot who agreed to fly me out. Despite the heavy layer of new snow, we could still make out my crew's trail. We followed it, and finally, I spotted the yellow Cat. It looked like the boys were putting some fill across the river, but the Cat was down in a swamp. We landed. "Well, Otis, everything went pretty good until we were backing up to get some more fill, and I backed out on a beaver dam hidden under the snow," Craig said.

Athabascan Natives, including a good friend of Craig's from the nearby village of Takotna, had come out to help. They had an old tractor, but that broke down when they tried to pull my dozer. I was stumped.

"There's a U.S. Army radar station nine miles up on top of the mountain here," said Craig's friend, "and I know the major pretty well. We can drive there in my truck and see if he can help. I know they've got a D-7 with a winch."

The major, a slim man with a narrow face, struck me as someone who'd go strictly by the rules. He seemed sympathetic but said the Army had regulations, and "helping miners isn't part of my job."

We talked some more. As we got up to leave, he said, "Well, come back tomorrow, boys. Maybe there's something I can do."

Thanks to the Takotna folks, we slept indoors that night on the floor of the Takotna village community center. That was lots warmer than bedding down with the machinery outdoors with temps well below zero—as my crew had been doing. We headed back up the mountain the next morning.

"I called around and got permission to bring our D-7 down to help the Natives get their tractor out of the river, as a positive public relations gesture," smiled the major. "Of course, while we're down there, we might as well help you fellows out, too."

The guy who drove their tractor down the mountain pulled our Cat free without any difficulty and rescued the Natives' tractor, too. The driver wouldn't take a dime for his trouble, so I invited him to have a drink with us at the bar in Takotna. There was cause for celebrating that night, and I popped for a couple of rounds of drinks for everyone.

As we stood around laughing and talking, I noticed a wrinkled woman with gray hair in braids staring at me.

"Otis, I want to talk to you," she said finally, crooking a finger at me. "You're going up to Bear Creek to take over Jim Hunter's mine?"

"That's right," I nodded.

"It's a very bad creek," she said, squinting her eyes. "It's got a hex on it. My name's Polly, and I went out there to cook for old Jim—and I never got paid. Worse yet, he bought a young gal from an Athabascan chief and never paid for her. Well, the chief put a hex on the mine. That mine will never be successful. Did you know that two of Jim's sons died out there? It's a bad hex, Otis. You'll see."

We feasted on moose steaks that night, and in the morning, Andy and Craig moved out with the equipment led by a guide from the town. The guide, Jack Hunter, turned out to be Jim's half-Native grandson, a happy-go-lucky joker minus a few teeth. I was in Takotna with no transportation, but around 10 A.M., in flew David Strant. He'd gotten wind of the trouble. It seemed like whenever I had difficulties, David showed up. This time, he gave me a ride back to McGrath. Then the weather turned bad, and there I stayed for seven days.

Wind rattled my cabin windows and swirled snow, creating a whiteout. I hoped Andy and Craig were okay and wished to heck I'd gone out on the trail with my crew instead of trying to follow them by airplane.

Meanwhile, I talked to the attorney in McGrath who'd handled the Bear Creek mine sale. He'd phoned several of my partners in International Falls and decided to come in on the mine with us. He had an airplane and offered to do some flying for us. His flying charges would be used to pay his share of the pool.

Finally, I got into the air and found my crew twelve miles from Bear Creek, just across the Folger River, but there was no place to land. So we flew to Craig's place to check on his family, which I'd intended to do often during the trip. I was relieved to see smoke coming out of the cabin chimney.

As soon as the plane shuddered to a stop on the hard snow, Craig's wife, Fran, ran out the door. She threw her arms around me and said, "Otis, am I ever glad to see you. Craig's five days late, and I've been worried." Two little kids followed her outside: I knew she'd had a long wait. After I told her that the crew was getting close to my camp, I headed back into McGrath to get my gear, but couldn't book another airplane for two days. The flights were all full. Luckily, David came to town, and I hitched a ride out to the mine with him. My "luck" included a side trip following a wolf pack into the mountains, and daredevil flying that put my stomach in my throat. My face matched the snow by the time we set down on the camp airstrip.

"Where the hell've you been, Otis?" asked Andy. "That Cat gets around quicker'n you in an airplane." He was smiling but looking pretty haggard. "Most nights we slept out with the machines," he said. "We had to leave 'em running: it got down to thirty-five below. Otis, that's one trip I don't care to make ever again!"

Andy had a pot of beans cooking on Jim's old barrel stove and a white enamel teapot puffed steam. "I sure hope you brought out some brandy," Andy grinned. "I've got the water ready for a hot one!"

We slept in the uninsulated camp shacks one night and might as well've been outdoors. The next night, we crowded into the tiny winter cabin Jim had built for himself at the edge of the camp. But we weren't the only occupants. When Andy swung open the door, he laughed.

"See, I've already got a mattress, Otis," he said, pointing at a bunk that mice had filled with seeds and tundra cotton.

We fired up the woodstove in the cabin. At last we got warmed up, and I dreamed of a Caterpillar tractor on ice.

CHAPTER 5

Getting Ready To Mine

It was mid-March, and we had our big machines at Bear Creek. We'd come out on top of that challenge. Next, we set off to get old Folger Field airstrip cleaned off with the bulldozer so a C119 could fly in with the pumps, oil, power unit, and the rest of the equipment. Folger Field, larger than our camp airstrip, lay farther away at the foot of Cripple Mountain and hadn't seen much use in years. It was in pretty rough shape with forty years' worth of trees and brush and deep washouts.

Meanwhile, Ace Airway landed on the small airstrip at our camp to deliver a dog and some equipment I'd stored with them. I'd seen the little black dog, Dingo, a mix of Norwegian elkhound and Labrador, tied to a tree in McGrath. I took a fancy to him, and it bothered me to see a pup tied up that way. Since he looked pretty bony, I'd stop by to give him something to eat.

One day the owner stepped out of his house. "If you like that dog so much, take him with you. I don't want him," he said. So Dingo joined our mining crew.

That air delivery also included our mail and a radio that would allow us to communicate between Anchorage and camp. Through the radio, we'd also be hooked up with phone service to anyplace we wanted to call. The radio would be our link to emergency help, which was critical since we didn't have an airplane of our own.

We added another man to our crew, Jim Wagner, a relative of the McGrath attorney who'd be doing some flying for us. Jim was a loner who'd spent a lot of time in the Bush and had a husky dog named Yuke. The days were getting longer and nights started warming up some. Andy and Jim got the radio set up in the main camp.

I was anxious to call Audrey and my investors, and to arrange to fly out to get food supplies. Before we got through to anyone, though, the radio went dead. We fiddled and fussed with it, but all we got from that new radio was static. Fortunately, we had an old radio that received the regular Bush radio station out of McGrath, but we couldn't send messages to the station or use our phone service hook-up.

By March 31, we had Folger Field in pretty decent shape. The attorney-pilot had said he'd fly his small plane into camp to pick me up by the twenty-fifth or so. Where was he? Timing was getting tight. I needed to arrange for a C119 to fly in with my big equipment and bring in the rest of the supplies before spring thaws set in. During thaws, the airstrips turn into quagmires. For about six weeks, no airplanes would be able to land.

On April 1, I worked and worked with the new radio—and finally sent a message out to anyone anywhere who could hear me. "Where are you?" asked a voice back. "At Bear Creek, fifty miles north of McGrath, and we need to communicate with McGrath." The radio receiving our message turned out to be way out on the Aleutian Islands chain. I gave them a message to relay to the attorney-pilot, and they did.

The next morning, while we listened to the 5 A.M. McGrath radio program, a Bush message came that our attorney-pilot would be out that day. But the guy didn't come in until the next morning. Jim and Dingo and Yuke stayed out at the camp; Andy and I flew back to town and caught a flight to Anchorage.

I called home to Mizpah and told Audrey and Tim to fly out as soon as possible. They arrived in Anchorage on April 4. Then we bought our summer supply of groceries for a tab of four thousand dollars. Money began to be a hassle. The chairman of White Wolf Mining hadn't yet set up a bank account in Anchorage, as we'd decided to do at the meeting in October. It got sticky dealing with people and having to bill everything through International Falls, Minnesota. And we were having trouble getting checks cashed because we were a new outfit. It turned out to be a blessing that I'd sold the truck in Anchorage: the business that bought the truck was willing to cash our checks.

"We need to get the Anchorage bank account set up," I said to the mining corporation chairman when I reached him on the phone. He said he would. "In the meantime, have bills sent to me, and I'll see they get paid," he said. I told him that wouldn't set too well with folks up here who'd never heard of White Wolf Mining or International Falls, Minnesota.

Next, I went to Gilford Air, a flight company that flies C119s into the Bush to deliver bulky supplies.

"I'll have to send a pilot up to look at the approach to the airfield and its condition before we can agree to fly your pumps and equipment in," the Gilford Air fellow told me. "Our airplanes carry about twelve tons of cargo and can't just put down anywhere."

So I chartered a small plane to fly the captain of the C119 up there, to the tune of about eight hundred dollars. That night, I stopped by Gilford Air to get the report: The approach was fine, but the field had to be longer and a lot smoother. The Gilford Air fellow told me I'd have to do more work on it, then pay to fly the captain out to look at it again.

I told Gilford Air that I really had to hold costs down. Was that second inspection trip really needed? "Well, I have something I want you to see," the man said. I spent half an hour looking at pictures of airplane crashes.

"Those people all thought they had their runways in good shape, and we took their word and went in," he said. "Two of those accidents were really bad crashes. On one of them, we lost our pilot *and* the airplane."

We talked a long while. I told him about our mining venture and my experience with big machinery and working the Livengood Road. Finally, he said he'd trust me to get the field ready, and they'd go ahead and fly in with the load.

"Since your airstrip lies at the foot of Cripple Mountain, once we start our approach, we've got to land," the captain made a point of telling me. "Once we start in, there's no way we can pull out of it and get over Cripple Mountain with our load."

"I have to get everything into the camp in the next week and a half, before the spring thaw sets in," I said. I figured it'd take two flights, and we scheduled the first flight to take place in eight days. It was agreed that I'd contact them by radio to let them know I had the airstrip ready.

Andy stayed in Anchorage to oversee the loading of the airplane. "Be sure that the power unit and one pump goes on the first load, along with the groceries and welding supplies," I told him. "That way, if something should happen and they don't get in with the second load, we'll still be able to do some mining."

At last, Audrey, Tim, and I headed out to Bear Creek. Our Ace Airway flight from McGrath to the camp was Audrey's first ride in a Bush airplane. She looked pretty serious.

"I'm beginning to wonder just what I've gotten myself in for," she said.

"To tell you the truth, Audrey, there's times I wonder that about myself," I said. We both laughed.

A gusty wind bounced the airplane around and gave us a rough landing. Alongside the Bear Creek camp runway stood a couple of old, tumbledown shacks. Audrey climbed out of the airplane, and her eyes widened. "My God, Otis, we can't live out here in those."

She was mighty relieved to find out that those shacks weren't our living quarters. Dingo and Yuke bounded up to us, with Jim close behind on snowshoes. He grabbed an armful of Audrey's luggage and started for the camp. "How far do we walk?" asked Audrey. I told her five miles. She shrugged and said, "That's not bad."

"Well, actually, it's more like three quarters of a mile," I said. She chuckled and answered, "That's better."

Having Audrey and her good-natured humor in camp would make a difference. Plus she'd seen the pictures I'd taken of the cook shack interior last fall and saw to it that we bought five gallons of white paint, tablecloths, and some curtains.

When Audrey walked into the old cookhouse, she just laughed. "Well, with a little paint and lots of elbow grease, I think it'll be okay, Otis," she said.

I got right to work on Folger Field. It was thawing some in the day but still freezing solid at night. I worked with the Cat, back-blading to get the airstrip smooth. I lengthened the runway out to about four thousand feet and made sure no trees interfered with the approach end. On April 16, David Strant stopped in.

"My radio's still balking," I told him. "Would you call Gilford Air and tell them I'm ready?"

David said, "Sure, and I'll have them send a Bush message to the McGrath radio station, telling you what day they are coming."

We got a message that Gilford Air would be in on the eighteenth, weather permitting. Lady Luck gave us a bright, sunny day on the eighteenth. Audrey packed sandwiches and the works, and we all went over to Folger Field to wait for the airplane. Obviously appreciative of our work, three rabbits were racing back and forth on the hard surface. We chuckled at the show, until it ended abruptly: the rabbits scattered when a lynx padded out of the trees. About an hour later, Tim poked my shoulder and pointed. At the end of the runway, two moose stood watching us.

We waited all day, but no airplane came.

"Well, what do we do now?" Audrey asked as we headed back to camp. "Come back tomorrow, I guess," I said.

We all went back to Folger Field the next day. The weather looked good, and about 10:30 A.M., we heard an airplane coming in. The plane flew high over Cripple Mountain, then started circling the field. Since we didn't have an air sock, we ignited a couple of old tires soaked in diesel fuel and got black smoke started as a wind indicator. The wind was just right: it was blowing down off the mountain so they'd be heading into it on their landing.

After two low passes, the C119 came down our valley on its final approach. I didn't look when the plane landed, not until I heard the props reverse and I knew the plane was okay and on the ground.

Andy got out of the plane, white-faced. "When we landed, the plane rattled so bad I thought it would split apart," he said. We opened the back of the airplane, and I saw the pickup we'd bought, the groceries, the oil and acetylene, and welding materials—but no pump or power unit! Andy had not followed my instructions. The pilot said he'd be back the next day with the rest of the equipment, and I hoped to heck the weather held up one more day.

We started hauling the groceries down to the cookhouse. "You forgot something, Andy," I said on the way down.

"Yes. I know. We didn't get the pump and power unit on," he said.

"Then I also want you to know that if it starts raining and the plane can't get in, we aren't going to be mining this summer. The only good thing I can say about this situation is that we will have plenty to eat."

That night, the radio weather forecaster predicted clouds and rain showers for the next day. That was bad news because the Folger Field airstrip was mainly ice and packed snow.

The forecast proved right. The next day was overcast with a fine rain coming down. When I went up to inspect Folger Field, a little water had started coming off from it. I didn't know what to do. If this kept up for another day, we'd be out of business for our mining season.

The rain stopped the next day, but the airstrip was not as good as it had been. That night, the radio had a message from Gilford Air. They'd be out in the morning. So, I headed back up to look at Folger Field. I stood out there and wondered how this would work out. To make matters worse, I couldn't contact Gilford Air with our out-of-commission radio. The pilot would just have to look the airstrip over from the air and decide whether or not to put down.

At least the next day was clear. At 1 P.M., we heard the airplane coming. Water was running down the airstrip when they circled over. I had a lump about the size of a baseball in my throat when the C119 started its final approach. Down it came, right on the approach end of the strip. All I could see was water flying, then the plane, safe on the ground.

The pilot caught sight of me and rolled down his window. "My friend, I knew it was important that you get your pumps out to the mine, but this is the last damn load I'm ever going to bring in here for you."

We unloaded the airplane, and it taxied clear to the end of the runway and was off the ground before it got halfway down the airstrip. I was mighty relieved to see it get off safely. So, I know, was the pilot.

At the supper table that night, I told the crew that we needed to take care of ourselves and not get hurt. We'd be isolated for probably six weeks—with no way to get out for help.

Our next chore was to cut firewood. We took one of the coal haulers down in the valley and spent a week cutting wood, piling it up, and splitting it. We were nearly out of wood at camp, and even during the summer, some of the evenings would be cold enough to need a fire. And by the middle of August, we'd be building fires every evening.

Then, with the camp in order and our firewood stacked, we were ready to mine for gold.

CHAPTER 6

On the Wild Side

Audrey started a diary when she came here. On April 30, 1982, she wrote: "Otis is stripping again. Made pineapple cake. Cloudy and cold—thirty-five degrees above at noon. Walked to upper camp—me, Dingo, and pistol. Going to leave pistol at home. More scared of it than bears."

By May 1, it was staying light nearly seventeen hours. I'd started stripping with the bulldozer, ripping off the frozen moss and tundra, getting ready to set in our big pumps and pipelines and our nozzles. We had ten to fifteen feet of overburden atop the gravel. I also made a ditch to get our water down from Cripple Creek along the hillside and into the mine. Meanwhile, I kept an eye out for the McGrath attorney-pilot's airplane bringing our mail. He'd have to drop it in a mail sack because the airstrip was too soft for him to land.

Right from the start, we all worked hard, including Audrey. She gave the cookhouse a thorough scrubbing, dressed it up with flowered oilcloth on the table and gingham curtains on the shelves, fed us homemade bread and hearty stews, and did the washing. It wasn't fun washing our grimy clothes outdoors in a gas-engine wringer washer and galvanized tubs. She took most things in stride and kept track of daily events.

Her May 5 diary entry read: "Fifteen degrees above at 6 A.M. Back to carrying pistol. Andy and boys went to Folger River for timber. They came across a pack of twenty to thirty wolves at Folger Field, only two and a half miles from here. My hand fit in the wolf's track. Craig came over by snowmobile and took my mail. Otis started platform for the sluice box. Baking cookies. Clear, windy."

To build an elevated sluice box that we could feed with a front-end loader, we needed to bring in some big timbers—big white spruce—from down by Folger River. So the boys took off with Jim's old crawler one morning to get the timbers. They were late returning.

About 8 P.M., I went outside to see if I could hear the Cat coming. Across the creek, I saw a big white wolf. I knew he was after Dingo. I went inside to get my rifle and came back, but he'd disappeared. Then he showed up at the end of a tailing pile. I fired my gun and he took off. When I went to where I'd seen him, I could tell by the tracks that he'd spent lots of time stalking back and forth—trying to get up close enough to get our dogs. About an hour later, the boys came in with the Cat, bursting to tell me that a pack of twenty to thirty wolves had come out and walked on the Cat trail. Some of the wolf tracks were four or five inches across the pad of their paws!

While I worked on stripping, Andy, Jim, and Tim were building the wooden frame for the sluice box out of the logs they'd brought in. It was a new type of sluice box, one that I wanted to experiment with, about thirty feet long and seven feet wide.

On May 21, Audrey wrote: "Andy fell through the glacier up to his armpits. Was he cold! Glacier dangerous now. Some places fifteen feet deep."

By late May, snow was melting and creeks flowed in

full force. Bear Creek ran alongside our mining site but wouldn't supply a lot of water in July and August, so I needed to get a reservoir in to hold the water we brought down from Cripple Creek. But where on earth, I wondered, was that attorney-pilot with our mail?

A pioneer spirit took hold of us: we trudged through the mud excited, looking forward to the day when we'd have our first cleanup. Cleanups are when you separate the dirt and gravel from the gold. From what Jim and I had mined last fall, we already had some material to put through, but our old dragline was a sorry-looking sight. Old Jim'd misjudged how high the glacier would rise. It was almost over the cab. I knew it'd be July before it thawed enough to even pull the dragline out of there. And there'd be damage from the ice and freezing.

Weeks passed and still no mail. The attorney-pilot hadn't come by even once. I wanted news from my White Wolf Mining officers! Tim hiked our outgoing mail over to the Strants' at Colorado Creek—a two-hour-plus walk—on Saturdays since that was his religious day off. After arriving at Bear Creek, with Andy and Audrey's help I'd written letters back to White Wolf Mining investors, for them to read at their meetings. They'd agreed to meet every month during the mining season, and I was to be mailed minutes of those board meetings.

One night, we heard an airplane coming in. It was David. He passed over and dropped a big mail sack at our cookhouse door.

News from the outside world! We had letters from all our kids—but nothing from White Wolf Mining. Our son Dave reported that things were bad on the farm. Markets were depressed and the weather'd been lousy in Mizpah. Audrey got upset about it, but I reminded her that we'd been through bad times on the farm, too. I told her not to worry, that hog prices would probably come up and things would work out. I don't know if she believed me or not.

That evening Tim walked up to the airstrip as he did

nearly every evening. This time he came back in a hurry.

"Otis, there's a flock of geese right on the end of the airstrip. Why don't we go up and see if we can get some?"

Audrey laughed. "Tim, you better let Otis tell you his story about hunting geese in Alaska."

"As far as I'm concerned, those geese can stay up there," I told Tim. "I don't want a goose haunting me like one did thirty years ago in Alaska."

"You're kidding me, Otis," Tim said.

"Nope," I answered. "There'll be no goose hunting in *this* mining camp."

Of course, I had to tell him the story. Back when Audrey and I were based along the Catalina River at the Livengood Road camp, geese would fly overhead, cruising the river every morning. Well, I shot one of a pair. The rest of the summer, the other goose flew alone over our camp, honking, looking for the mate. Then someone told me that geese mate for life! Sure enough, the next summer, that lone goose returned to fly over our camp, honking and honking. That put an end to my goose hunting.

Tim went off shaking his head and told the rest of the crew. They had a good laugh over it, but no one shot any geese at our camp.

David delivered our mail for the next few weeks, always dropping the mail sack at the cookhouse door. Nothing came from White Wolf Mining. The ground started drying up then, so an airplane could land. One evening, David's plane set down on the airstrip, proof that it was indeed dry enough for landing. I thanked him for being our mailman since our attorney-pilot had reneged on his deal to deliver our mail.

That summer we watched the tundra come to life. One sunny day, after Audrey walked out to our work site with lunch, she and I went on a hike up to the airstrip. A soft southern breeze warmed the air; pink and yellow flowers bloomed beside the trail; and tundra cotton put a fluffy white blanket on the hills.

"It's beautiful out here, Otis," Audrey said. We rounded

a bend and watched a brown-feathered ptarmigan cross the trail with eight or ten chicks. Life seemed awfully good that afternoon, except for a nagging uneasiness I couldn't shake. I thought about the ptarmigan: not many of those chicks would escape stealthy lynx and other predators. Gold miners had about the same chance of making it out here in the Bush.

That night, when Audrey and I got ready for bed, I told her that something was really bothering me.

"In all this time, I haven't heard one word from White Wolf Mining. No minutes of meetings and no financial statement. I don't know how much money the corporation really has! And I know my crew will be wanting to get paid."

Talking about it helped a little. Finally, we got our radio to work fairly well and I made contact with Anchorage. Then I called a partner in International Falls and asked him what was going on.

"Yes, the money's in the bank, but I'm not sure of the amount," he told me.

"I want you to go to the bank and send me a complete statement," I said. "I need to know what's been deposited and how much money we've really got." He said he'd do that.

By the fifth of June, it was daylight twenty-four hours a day. Audrey's diary entries said: "June 7. It's fifty-six degrees at 3 P.M. Another lonely day. I miss my kids and friends. I found a bird's nest today. I guess I'll watch that. Made bread. Partly cloudy and still it rains.

"June 10. At 8 A.M., fifty-five degrees, clear and warm. First day without long sleeves and with no fire. Also had company. David and Jack Hunter were here for coffee. Wonder if there are any females around this place? At 4:30 P.M., cloudy and sixty degrees.

"June 13. Clear and fifty-six degrees at 6 A.M. This is a Sunday. No big deal out here. Been at Bear Creek more than eight weeks. It seems like a hundred years! Put water in barrels for the cookhouse. Rain and hail at 7 P.M."

A little past the middle of June, Tim and I tried to run some lines on some of the claims. That meant we had to walk out of the cut and go into the tundra and small spruce. We started blazing our way up there. I was running a compass behind Tim, looked up, and saw that his red shirt had turned gray. He was covered with mosquitoes. Suddenly, they were everywhere—in our ears, eyes, and nose, hanging on Tim's beard. Huge and hungry, these mosquitoes were the worst I'd ever seen—and Minnesota mosquitoes can be plenty fierce. Tim looked at me and I looked at him. We shook our heads and took off at a run back down into the cut. There, they left us alone.

The boys and I were putting in many fourteen- and sixteen-hour days. We had to push hard due to the short mining season. Audrey always got up early to make breakfast and get lunches ready for the day. One morning, she came tearing back into the bedroom.

"You've got a visitor, Otis," she whispered. "He's looking in the kitchen window."

I knew exactly what she meant: we had our first bear of the season. Once a bear comes in, you're well advised to shoot him or put up with return visits, a ransacked camp, and maybe somebody getting maimed or killed. We couldn't afford to take that chance. I grabbed my 30.06, slipped outside, and met the fellow face to face when he came 'round the corner of the cookhouse—about three hundred pounds of black bear.

I shot him. The boys came bounding out of the bunkhouse moments later.

"He's a big one," said Tim, bending down to run a hand over the bear's coarse, black coat.

I nodded. "Yep. Better stay on our toes and keep our guns loaded. We'll have more before the season's end."

That got the morning off to a lively start. The boys and I dug a grave and buried the bear. I knew other surprises waited for us. As it turned out, wild critters proved less troublesome than the wiles of nature and mankind.

CHAPTER 7

Keeping Above Water

At the end of June, we gained another worker. Brent, who'd come out with Tim last fall, showed up with his big dog, Dillon. I welcomed the extra help. Little did I know then that I'd soon end up shorthanded!

Our plan was to start sluicing for gold around the tenth of July. David said he usually started then. The ground would be thawed enough to let us get down to the gravel above the bedrock, which is where you find the gold in placer mining. After the ground has been stripped down to the permafrost level, you've got to clean away the overburden to about a foot or so above the decomposed-bedrock gravel. That involves cutting channels in the ice and muck to aid in thawing, then hooking up giants by pipelines to a big pump which takes water from your reservoir. The giants shoot water out of high-pressure nozzles—about five thousand gallons a minute—and the ice and muck washes away through a drain ditch that leads to your creek.

Then you sluice, scooping up the gravel and continuously feeding it into the sluice box using a front-end loader. Meanwhile, you flush water over the debris in the sluice box, about two thousand gallons per minute. The sluice box has rug-like mats on the bottom. Atop that are riffles—two-inch-high bars, four inches apart, set into the box in four-foot sections. On top of the riffles go punch plates with one-inch-diameter holes. The gold and finer material pass through those holes and get trapped in the riffles in the bottom of the box. The gold is taken out of the box at cleanup.

We kept on with our stripping, and the Fourth of July rolled around. The attorney-pilot from McGrath flew in with our mail and the makings for a celebration—a forty-pound salmon, pop, and beer—the first I'd seen of him in a long while. We'd moved the sluice box that morning and planned on working all day. But Jim said, "Say, Otis, why don't you let me barbecue that salmon for us?"

"What are you going to use for a barbecue?" I asked.

"You'll see," he grinned.

"Go ahead, Jim," I said. "You boys can take the rest of the day off. We could use some time to rest up."

Right off, Jim headed for the sauna the boys had rigged up earlier that season. They'd built a ten-by-twelve-foot shack and put in a barrel stove with a stovepipe and door. Then they piled rocks over the stove and atop the rocks, they set another barrel filled with water. You'd fire the stove with dry spruce; when the water boiled, you'd dip it out on the rocks. It got hot and steamy in there, and it worked pretty well. We put in little racks to sit on and got another barrel for cold water to douse yourself after you'd steamed awhile.

Jim fired up the sauna, got himself cleaned up, and put on fresh clothes. Then he put a grill over some rocks outside the cookhouse and got tree bark to use for coals.

A little while later, someone yelled, "The sauna's on fire!" I looked and sure enough, the door was open and black smoke was pouring out. I couldn't see Jim anywhere around.

Andy came running up with a bucket of icy glacier water he'd fetched from the creek and heaved the water in the door—just as Jim stepped out of the sauna. He spluttered and yelled. Meanwhile flames started dancing on the sauna roof. We all ran for water and finally got the roof wet down. Jim stood there, dripping and muttering. "Andy, you should be more careful where you toss water," he said.

"Oh, well, you always rinse off with cold water after a sauna," Andy teased.

"Not with my clothes on," Jim said.

Audrey watched from the cookhouse. She was laughing when I walked in.

"I thought you fellows were going to rest," she grinned. "That didn't look very restful to me. But whatever Jim's doing with the salmon out there, it sure does smell good."

The sauna was saved, and Jim finished barbecuing his salmon. That salmon really did taste good. We went back to work the next day and finally got the sluice box put in place and the pipelines set up. We were ready to go!

Sluicing started on July 7. Every time we shut down for something, we'd all jump in the sluice box and look for gold.

"There's gold showin' up! There's gold in here!" we'd yell. It sure made me grin.

On July 8, Audrey wrote in her diary: "Clear and hot at 6 A.M. It can get to eighty degrees in this valley. The sluice box works, but the loader doesn't. More trouble."

On July 9: "Rain. Got the loader to work halfway. David came last night. Gold is in the riffles."

I liked seeing that gold in the box. Even problems with the loader didn't dampen my high spirits, but lack of communication with White Wolf Mining did. Because I'd not received the promised financial statements, the crew hadn't received any paychecks yet. I told them I was waiting to hear from International Falls. The boys were good about it, but I didn't like it. I had in the back of my mind that I'd at least be able to get cash for the gold and pay the guys their wages.

On the twelfth of July, a small plane came in. It was the attorney-pilot from McGrath. We were busy sluicing. He walked up to where I was standing in the sluice box and asked, "How are things going?"

"Things are going well out here, but things aren't going so well between you and me, or between me and my board back in International Falls. We're going to be out of fuel in five days. One of my partners said he'd mail me a financial statement, but he didn't—so I don't know if I've got money to buy more fuel. And you promised to fly the mail in and you haven't been doing that regularly."

The fellow hemmed and hawed. He said things had gotten very busy, then the weather acted up. He had lots of reasons why he hadn't been able to bring the mail. I listened, and then asked that he give me a ride to McGrath so I could telephone the White Wolf Mining accountant.

He agreed to fly me to McGrath. We shut down the sluice box, and like everybody else, the attorney-pilot climbed into the box and inspected the riffles. "Be damned if you don't have a lot of gold here, Otis," he said. I nodded. We had a hefty show of very fine gold mixed in with black sand.

In McGrath, I went to the pay phone in the bar and called the accountant who was the treasurer of the White Wolf Mining Corporation.

"I need the statements through the past months right away," I told him. He told me to go ahead and write checks for my crew. There was enough money there for that. Then I asked, "Well, what about buying more fuel?"

The problem was, according to him, that some of the investors who'd made commitments to White Wolf Mining were holding out. That didn't set well with me.

"Tell them we'll be having a cleanup in a couple of weeks, and there is gold in the sluice box. Maybe that'll encourage them to meet their commitment," I said.

The accountant said that statements would be mailed to us the next day. That evening, I flew back to camp with the attorney-pilot, wondering if I really would receive the bank statements. Based on past performance of board members, I sure wasn't holding my breath, but I didn't want to write paychecks until I got a look at the bank statements.

After we got into the air, the attorney-pilot started talking. "Otis, I'm sorry that I didn't get the mail to you the way I promised I would," he said.

"It did cause us some hardships," I answered. "It was my understanding that you'd agreed to fly for us as payment for your shares in the mine, plus some additional cash. The accountant told me you haven't paid anything in yet. It looks to me like you and some of the other investors are playing a pretty close poker game—waiting for other investors to furnish the money to put gold in the sluice box and then come in safely afterwards."

"Well, Otis, I've got a proposition that I think will interest you. There's a 207 owned by the Native corporation that has a fuel tank in it and is available, and I know a pilot who's looking for a flying job. How about if I contact the pilot, and we start flying in fuel to you? That should pay for my shares."

It was the best option I had at the moment. "Okay, fellow, you've got a deal," I said. A few days later, the pilot, a gutsy fellow called Shany West, started flying in a hundred gallons of fuel at a time to keep our operation going.

We got a message over the McGrath radio station that company was coming to visit the Hahns. A couple of days later, Ace Airway flew in with my brother Ray, his wife, June, my cousin Bernita, and her husband, Harry.

I drove the front-end loader to the strip to pick them up, and we all started laughing and talking at the same time. The women climbed in the cab with me. The men climbed into the loader's bucket with the luggage and we jounced our way down to the camp. Ray'd brought in fresh steaks, roast beef, and a couple of gallons of milk—a real treat for us.

Audrey and June and Bernita talked steadily for a couple

of days. I know Audrey appreciated having some females around, not to mention extra hands in the kitchen. Meanwhile, Ray and Harry pitched in around camp and got Jim's old light plant working. Now we could have electric lights for a couple of hours each night when darkness set in.

Harry, a large man who ran a successful hog-farming operation in Illinois, always liked to kid around. But he was serious when he asked me if I'd sell my dog, Dingo. He'd taken a liking to that odd little dog.

"I don't know, Harry," I said. "I guess I could sell him, but he's a rare Alaskan Dingo breed. There aren't many of them left, maybe twenty in all. I bought him because Dingos are good bear dogs. I don't think you'd want to pay the price I'd have to ask."

"How much?" Harry asked.

"Well, at least seven hundred dollars," I said.

After supper, Harry took Bernita aside and asked her if it'd be okay with her if he bought Dingo for seven hundred dollars and took him home with them. Well, I saw Ray sitting across the table smirking. Audrey started laughing and said, "Harry, I think I'd better tell you that Otis's Dingo is nothing but a mongrel some guy gave him in McGrath."

We all had a good laugh.

"Well, Otis, you sure had me believing you on that one," Harry said.

The day before they left, I went outside and saw Bernita standing there alone, staring at the mountains.

"It's quite a place, isn't it?" I said.

She nodded. "I just wanted to get one final look at the last frontier in the United States," she told me. It seemed quiet around the place when they left.

One night, David came over to our camp. "Fellas, I'm going to have my first cleanup," he announced. "Would you like to come over and help with it?"

We owed David a lot—all the flying me around he'd done and dropping our mail. He wouldn't take pay for any of that. I said, "Absolutely. The whole crew will be over. We'll be more than glad to help you with the cleanup."

Over at Colorado Creek, they always had a wager on the amount of gold they'd get in each cleanup. I guessed 284 ounces. When the cleanup started on the first ten feet of take, after the sand and gravel had been worked off it, that ten feet shimmered yellow with gold. *I'm sure gonna be a long ways off,* I thought. But the farther down the box we went, less and less gold showed up. The first ten feet are often the best part of the take. His box was about forty feet long.

After David took the gold out of the box, he still had lots of work to get the black sand out of it and get it ready to market. He wouldn't have a count on the gold until then.

"Hey, Otis, let's have our cleanup," said Andy when we got back from David's. Everyone was itching to see what we had after the Strant cleanup. But I wanted to sluice another five, six days into our box before the cleanup. I'd opened up some ground at the side of our cut where, in panning, I'd get between forty and fifty colors (flakes or particles), which is very good. I wanted that little piece of ground in the box!

On July 16, heavy rainclouds moved in. It was raining hard in the valley up above us, although we weren't getting much rain. It worried me. I'd been warned about flash floods. That's why we built our sluice box on skids—so we could move it quickly.

The next morning rainclouds still hugged the valley. I went up to look at the reservoir. It was almost full, even with our big pump running. Water was coming up fast, and our overflow wasn't handling the water. I checked on the reservoir every half hour: the water kept rising.

"Let's get the pipeline down and pull the box to high ground," I yelled to the boys. Slipping and sliding in the mud, the boys wrestled with the unwieldy pipeline. I hooked the Cat up to the sluice box and inched it up to higher ground. By the time we got the box moved, the water had risen above my big pump. This was serious! I couldn't afford to lose our pump and power unit!

"Stand clear," I shouted to the crew. I climbed back on the dozer, lowered the blade, and cut an opening in the reservoir below the pump. I saw that Tim was still in the cut, struggling with the pipeline.

"Let the pipeline go and get the hell out of there," I yelled. He dropped the pipe and leaped up on the bank seconds before a mighty whoosh of chocolate-tinted water flooded the whole cut. Jim was out in the middle of it, lugging our toolbox from the opposite bank. "Forget the toolbox, Jim. Just get out of the cut," I shouted. But he hung on to it, slowly, slowly making his way over to us, water up past his hips and rising fast.

Brent's golden retriever, Dillon, barked at us from across the creek. We saw him leap into the water, trying to swim over to us, but the current swept him down the swollen creek.

"Oh, no!" Brent said, "It looks like I'm going to lose my dog."

Mud-drenched and exhausted, we watched the swirling floodwater. The ground I'd figured on putting into the sluice box was suddenly under seven to eight feet of gravel, and the drains were full. My shoulders and arms throbbed. Andy, Tim, Jim, and Brent just stood beside the sluice box, staring at the water. No one talked.

Suddenly, the clouds lifted, replaced by a bright, sunny, blue sky. Within three hours, the floodwaters had started to recede. The cut was a muddy mess, and part of the pipeline was gone. From the looks on the boys' faces, they thought the flood had finished our mining venture. Tim asked me, "Well, what do we do now, Otis? Go home?"

"I'm afraid you boys aren't going to get off that easy," I said. "We've had a setback, that's for sure, but we're a long way from being licked."

Late that afternoon, the boys headed for the bunkhouse to get cleaned up. I heard a shout so went to investigate.

There sat Dillon, wet and muddy and tired, in the middle of Tim's bunk. "Hey, am I glad to see you, fellow!" Brent beamed. Tim grumbled, "I just wish he'd picked *your* bunk to sit on."

David flew in the next day and walked into the camp.

"Otis, I've been worried about you," he said. "I figured maybe you'd even lost your sluice box in the flood."

"We're not that bad off, but some of the ground I wanted to sluice is lost beneath the gravel and muck," I said. We headed for the cookhouse and Audrey set out mugs of coffee and sugar cookies.

"Old Jim weathered his share of floods here, too, Otis," David said. "And you must have a miner's feel for gold. We got the results of our cleanup—287 ounces. You were only three ounces short on your guess. That's damn close!"

"So, what do you plan to do next?" Audrey asked me when David left.

"The first thing is to restore the reservoir," I said, sipping coffee and thinking. "When the water's gone, we'll hook up the pipeline and put the box back in the cut a little farther. There's some ground there I can put through."

I tried to sound more enthusiastic than I felt. The flood left all of us pretty low for a couple of days. We tried to get the old dragline set up to clean out the drains but that didn't work out. Andy and Brent set to moving one of the big pumps with the front-end loader. I was working on the sluice box when I heard the scream. Good God! Brent was pinned between the loader and the pump!

They had a short chain hitching the loader to the pump. When Andy stopped the loader and got off, Brent had stepped between the pump and loader. The loader slipped backwards, trapping Brent. My heart thumped as I watched Andy leap back up on the loader. I wanted to shout, "Slow down, Andy, be sure you don't shove that engine into reverse," but the words stuck in my throat. When the loader pulled forward, Brent crumpled to the ground.

We've had our first taste of that damn bad luck hex, I thought as I raced over to Brent. He was white-faced, struggling to breathe. Gradually, his breathing eased. He could move his limbs. We helped him into camp and into bed. I told him I was going to try to radio for help. Brent was talking by then and said, "Wait up, Otis. Give me a little while to rest. I think I'm going to be okay."

A half hour passed. Then Brent worked himself into sitting up.

"I think I just got squeezed real good, Otis," he said.

The next day, he was black and blue from his shoulders to his toes.

After the flood, I began to notice some changes in Andy. He started coming in late for breakfast and was pulling back a little bit. It was troublesome to me because I relied heavily on Andy as our mechanic and bookkeeper. I feared that the extra-long workdays were getting to him. Mining is something not everyone's cut out to do.

One morning Jim came in and told me, "I think that Andy's going to go to town. Shany West is coming in with fuel this afternoon, and Andy's in the bunkhouse getting ready to fly to McGrath."

I went up to the bunkhouse. Andy was dressed in clean jeans and a new-looking plaid shirt.

"I hear you're going to town, Andy," I said. "Do you recall when I hired you that I wondered how you'd feel about being a miner when the going got tough like it is now?"

Andy sat down on his bunk and studied the floor.

"Well, I was worried that you might pull out on us," I said. "If you leave now, you might as well not come back. We'll just have to get along without you."

"I thought you appreciated how hard I've worked and all the bookkeeping I've done for you, Otis," Andy responded, raising his head and meeting my eyes.

"Well, Andy, I do. You have worked hard. But everyone here has worked just as hard."

We talked back and forth awhile longer.

"I'll stay on, Otis," Andy finally said.

At last, we got our equipment hooked up. To get caught up, we started sluicing night and day. Since we were working in lower-grade ground, I wanted to work more ground to improve our take. On the night that Andy was going to take the P.M. shift, Shany West came in with a delivery— which included some booze. I noticed that Andy took a bottle out with him when he left for his shift.

I went out before he started up the loader. "That's strictly against my policy, Andy," I said, hearing the strain of the past week in my voice. "Maybe you'd better just go to town. You won't be any good to us behaving this way."

Andy got off the loader and walked back into the camp. He hitched a ride with Shany West and ended up in Anchorage. I was disappointed. I felt bad for Andy, for myself, and for the boys. His departure meant extra work for the whole crew.

Then another flood hit before we started our cleanup. Things were pretty tense around the camp, with long work shifts and tempers starting to flare.

It was even starting to get to Jim, ordinarily a stoic individual. One night Brent's dog, Dillon, and Jim's husky, Yuke, started snarling and fighting outside the cookhouse door. Brent ran out, grabbed on to Dillon, and kicked Yuke away. Jim stepped up to Brent, eyes narrowed, and said, "Nobody kicks my dog." Brent had the good sense to keep hold of Dillon and walk away. None of us knew much about Jim, except that he wore a shoulder holster. He seemed the sort of fellow who wouldn't back down easily.

By now, the strain was affecting all of us. Audrey wrote in her diary on August 1: "Getting set back up after the flood. Washing clothes. God help us in this mine."

CHAPTER 8

Cleanup!

"Andy wants to come back, Otis." Shany West delivered that message along with the next load of fuel.

"Tell him I said 'No deal,'" I replied.

But when Shany brought the same message the next trip, I hesitated before I shook my head. I needed as many workers as I could get. And I, after all, was responsible for bringing him to Alaska. I knew he'd pulled his own weight most of the time, and he had worked a couple of months without any pay.

"You've been awfully quiet tonight, Otis," Audrey said while she washed dishes after supper one night. "Are you thinking about giving Andy another chance?"

"You know me pretty well, don't you?" I said.

"I guess I do." She refilled my coffee cup and gave my shoulder a squeeze.

On Shany West's next trip, I told him to tell Andy there'd be a place for him if he wanted back on the mining crew. And back he came.

"I hope this works out, Andy," I told him when he walked into camp. "It will, Otis," he said. I had a few reservations: Andy did like his occasional party. But I really wanted to believe him.

At last, we had our first cleanup. Old Jim Hunter had Ace Airway drop him off that morning. After we sluiced the material through, we took out the punch plates and raised the riffles, rinsing them with a hose. Next, we took out the mats, shook them out, and rolled them up. We'd get the residue of extra-fine gold out of them later. Then we started shoveling the leavings forward in the box. It was tough washing out all the mud. We did that by getting in the box and paddling the stuff with boards while we ran water over it. At first, the water that came out of the end of the box was almost pure mud. After an hour or so of washing, when the water finally ran clear, we spread the remaining material out in the box. Then we washed very slowly, moving the material around, trying to get the gold to settle. Finally, a fine line of gold began to settle in the bottom of the box. We picked that up, and repeated the slow washing process over and over again.

Jim perched on the edge of the sluice box up at the front, his old wool shirt half open and the green Hahn Harvester cap I gave him last year sitting cockeyed on his head.

"Come on up here, Otis," he yelled during the washing. "We've got gold coming already!" In midafternoon, the Ace Airway plane put down. Jim muttered about having to leave before the finish of the cleanup. I walked him to the airstrip, noticing he was a little less sure on his feet these days.

We stood beside the airplane, and Jim shook my hand. "Otis, I probably won't get out for all the cleanups. You can hold my percentage for me 'til you get to town," he said.

I watched his eyes start to fill up. "I trust you, Otis. This was my place and my country for forty years. Every time I come out here, it gets harder and harder to leave."

The airplane pilot told him to hurry. The weather was closing in over the Sunshine Mountains. The old fellow kicked his heels together to knock the mud off his boots, as he must have done a million times.

"I wish you well, Otis," he said and climbed into the plane.

"There sure enough is lots of gold in here," Tim grinned when I got back to the sluice box.

"Yes," I agreed, "but I'd like it better if it wasn't mixed in with that black sand."

The black sand—a type of magnetite—stuck to the gold like a second skin. I studied it and shook my head. We'd have to do something besides washing to separate the sand and gold. You couldn't even pan it by hand and separate it! I'd have to come up with some other technique. In the meantime, I decided to put the gold and sand in barrels so I could get the box back together and get on with the sluicing.

My new type of sluice box was a disappointment. In fact, its extra width slowed our first cleanup considerably. So we inserted a divider that narrowed the box to a four-foot width before we moved east to new ground that I'd stripped. That ground looked pretty good. We were getting coarser gold there.

When I came into camp to pick up some tools, I saw a big, gray malamute dog nosing around. I recognized her as one of the dogs from the Colorado Creek mining camp.

"You've got company," I told Audrey.

She said, "I know. She's my only female friend out here. She stops by for a visit every now and then."

One evening we came in after working all day in sleet and rain with a cruel north wind, and Audrey had a feast ready for us—fried chicken, mashed potatoes, gravy, and cinnamon rolls. That night, we put extra wood in the barrel stove before we went to bed. I fell asleep listening to the wind and sleet pounding on the tin roof of the old cookhouse. About 3 A.M., Audrey shook me awake.

"I think we've got a bear at the cookhouse door," she said, handing me my gun. I could hear some scratching, but it didn't sound like a bear to me. I inched the kitchen door open. Standing out there was that malamute dog, soaking wet.

"Poor thing. Let her come in," Audrey said.

I shook my head. "No. She doesn't live here, Audrey. And those dogs can stand this kind of weather."

"But it's such a nasty night, Otis."

I looked at Audrey's face and opened the door for her friend. In the dog came, shook herself, and gave the cookhouse a shower. Audrey put down a blanket for her by the stove, and we went back to bed.

Crash! My eyes flew open. Audrey bolted out of bed. I grabbed a flashlight. Dishes and pots were scattered everywhere. The whole cupboard had been knocked to the ground, and in the middle of the mess stood that malamute, gobbling a piece of fried chicken.

"Oh, no!" Audrey said. "I forgot that I put a piece of chicken on a plate and set it in the cupboard."

We spent the next hour cleaning up the place, and then it was time to fix breakfast.

"If I were you, Audrey, I'd have a hard time calling that dog my friend," I said.

A few days after we started sluicing again, Audrey took a phone message that a White Wolf Mining Corporation investor named Gene Bradley was in McGrath. He was heading out to see the operation. That was good news to me.

But there was bad news, too. In the last few weeks, Audrey had not been feeling well. I was worried about her. To make matters worse, our radio didn't work well. I couldn't count on it if we needed to call for emergency help. So we decided that she should go out when Shany West next came in, and fly back to Minnesota for medical care.

On the day that Gene was to arrive, Shany West flew in. Audrey and I held hands on the way to the airstrip. A lump grew in my throat as I watched her get on the airplane. The camp would be a lonely place without her.

It had clouded up and started to rain, and I took my time walking back. There was lots to do, but I didn't feel much like tackling it.

That afternoon, Gene flew in. He's a talkative fellow, about five feet, ten inches tall with salt-and-pepper hair.

Right off, as soon as we shook hands at the airstrip, he handed me a check for ten thousand dollars.

"Otis, we investors know that you're not getting the cooperation you should have from our end. We just don't know what to do about it yet. This check will give you some money to work with, in case you get in real trouble out here," he said.

"What about the payroll?" I asked him on the walk to the camp.

"I'd suggest you pay the workers a percentage of what is owed now, and when you get the gold out, pay them the rest." (And that's what I did.)

We also talked about how things were progressing. "We're getting gold, but right now our loader is broken down," I said. "I've gotten a message out to the Oregon tractor dealer who sold the loader to me. The dealer is bringing a mechanic out with him to see what's wrong with the motor. That was part of the guarantee when I purchased the loader; now I'll find out if the dealer meant what he said. It's a long way out here!"

Gene brought the bank drafts and statements from the bank. That night, he, Andy, and I sat at the table in the cookhouse and looked at all of that by flickering lantern light.

"A couple of these canceled checks don't make sense to me, Gene," I said. "Where are the minutes from the meetings when the board discussed and approved those particular expenditures?"

Gene said, "Well, those expenditures haven't been discussed in any meetings. You're president of the corporation, Otis. I'd say it's up to you to do what you feel you need to do about the questions you have when you return this fall."

Gene got a firsthand look at the gold in the sluice box, but with our loader out of commission, he didn't get to see any sluicing. Before he left, the tractor dealer flew in with a mechanic. They tried the loader out and told me that the torque converter had gone completely out of it. He'd send a new one up to me for Andy to put in. No problem with that, as Andy was knowledgeable about this type of transmission.

Gene went back to Minnesota, and the new torque converter arrived. Andy and I got it into the loader, and we went back to sluicing.

Our next cleanup looked really good but we still had trouble getting the gold out of the black sand. I thought about asking David Strant to come over and help us, but I didn't. It was getting late in the season, and he had plenty to do. Instead, I put the sand/gold mix in barrels as we did before. Then I decided to try a tip Old Jim'd given me: to use a cement mixer and mercury, which attracts the gold. Jim had run into similar problems. He suggested putting the material in the mixer along with mercury, hot water, and detergent. That'd worked for him.

We had a cement mixer at the camp already. When Shany West flew in with fuel, I asked him to go to Anchorage and pick up mercury, a gold wheel (which also aids in separating gold from sand), and a small electric generator to run the gold wheel. I figured I had about eight thousand dollars in the International Falls account, and I gave West two signed checks to pay for the gold wheel, generator, and mercury.

The weather turned pretty bad for two days. On the second night, I got hold of Shany West on our radio and asked him where the equipment was.

"I got over the Sunshine Mountains today," he said, "but your valley was completely fogged in. I'm going to try it again in the morning."

The next day brought fog and rain. About nine that evening, I heard an airplane go over pretty high. I figured it surely wouldn't be West out flying in this kind of weather.

The next morning, a bush pilot set down on our airstrip. Tim and Jim took off for the airstrip to find out what was up.

"That was a pilot named Lucky. He told us Shany West is missing," Jim reported to me. "The last radio contact with him said he was somewhere in our area with only ten minutes of fuel. He was going to have to go down."

West's chances weren't good, I knew. The fog lay close to the ground; he'd have a hard time picking his way through it to find a landing spot. Later we heard on the radio that he'd been missing since eleven the previous night, and a search was under way. Maybe that was his plane we had heard.

Around noon, the weather began to clear and the sun came out. We heard airplanes flying over, searching for Shany West. I figured the guy was a goner, done in by his crazy risk-taking. I'd gotten kind of fond of the character. I'd miss him. And I knew that when he went down in his plane so did our gold wheel, mercury, and generator.

David Strant came flying in that night. "That crazy Shany West went down last night," he told me.

"So we heard," I said. "It doesn't look good for him, does it?"

"Don't get all choked up, Otis," David said. He grinned. "I found Shany alive and well down in the flats. I listened to tapes Lucky had of Shany's last radio message. It sounded to me like that's where he'd be, so I flew out and landed on a sandbar at the flats. Sure enough, there was Shany West, and he had your gold wheel with him! His airplane's wrecked but be damned if he isn't determined to deliver that wheel like he said he would."

The next day, Shany West came roaring over the camp in the airplane he used to deliver fuel. In addition to fuel, he brought the gold wheel and the mercury. The bad news: he'd tossed the generator out to lighten the plane before he crashed. Well, I had to admit that I was happy to see him.

"If I were you, I think I'd have taken a day or two off after the crash," I said.

Shany shook his head. "Otis, if I hadn't got back in a pilot seat this morning, I'd probably never have flown an airplane again."

While we were waiting on the delivery from Shany West, Andy devised a retorting rig for recovering the mercury from the gold when it came out of the cement mixer. Andy's retorting device consisted of a cast iron pot set in a five-gallon barrel. Around the pot, he put sand and gravel. He used a hose to hook the barrel up to a propane tank and the propane to heat the barrel to five hundred degrees—that's what it takes to vaporize the mercury. Coming out of the top of the barrel was a pipe that ran down to a can. He enclosed the lower part of that pipe in a water manifold pipe which would circulate water to cool the mercury. When the mercury vapor reached the water-cooled segment of pipe, it returned to its liquid state and ran into the can.

"Well, what do you think we'll find inside?" I asked the boys before I opened the retorting device the first time we used it. No one said a word; they just watched me. I jerked off the cover.

"Wahoo!!" Adrenaline rushed through me. "We got ourselves some mighty pretty gold, boys!" I shouted. They took a look—and shouted, too.

"Andy, you've created one hell of a fine retorter," I said, pumping his hand.

Andy's invention worked better than we had hoped it would. After we ran the cement mixer for thirty to forty-five minutes, I'd pan out the balls of mercury loaded with gold. Those mercury balls went into the retort device. We let the retorter cool after we got all the mercury out of it. Then we'd remove the cover to admire a gleaming gold ingot.

We harvested the prettiest ingots you'd ever hope to see. After we separated the gold from the black sand that I'd put into barrels in our first cleanups and retorted the gold, we got something like 120 ounces of good gold. Later, when we took our gold to buyers, they said it was some of the nicest retorted gold they'd handled.

A few days after I'd retorted the material from the barrels, David picked me up in his Super Cub, and we flew to Fairbanks to market our gold. The wind was blowing hard, so David made the three-hour-plus flight at low level. We passed over herds of moose and caribou, beaver dams, lakes with geese and a few swans. It turned out to be an Alaska wilderness excursion.

That afternoon, when I left the gold buyer, White Wolf Mining was richer by some fifty thousand dollars. I was excited! I could hardly wait to tell the investors. So I went to a phone and called the White Wolf Mining chairman in International Falls. But his secretary said he was unable to talk to me then.

"That's too bad," I said, feeling real disappointment. "I've got news for him. Let him know that a check for fifty thousand dollars for our first gold sale is being mailed directly to him for our White Wolf Mining account."

On the flight home, we followed the Kuskokwim River, spotting moose hunters along the way. It was moose hunting season. We rounded a big bend in the river, and David said, "Look down there, Otis. I think a bear's got a kill. Let's get a closer look."

We buzzed low over the bear. Some moose hunters had quartered a moose and put it up on poles. Well, on top of the poles sat this brown bear, eating away. As we flew on, we saw the hunters packing in from the river to pick up their moose. We laughed. Those fellows were in for a little surprise.

Of course, the Bush holds lots of surprises. A few days later, I was in bed when I heard tin rattling on the side of the cookhouse. Dingo always slept in the front part of the cookhouse. All of a sudden, he let out a yelp, ran into the bedroom, and slid under the bed.

I grabbed my rifle and my old two-cell flashlight, wishing the batteries were stronger, and tiptoed to the door. I eased the wooden door open and shone my flashlight through the screen door: Bear! Up so close to the door I could smell him. But in the darkness, with my weak light, about all I could make out was the bear's face. I stepped back and fired.

That bear took off. I closed the wooden door fast and looked out the window. I could see a lantern still on in the bunkhouse, and heard one of the boys shout, "Did you get him?" Next I heard a scream and lots of shouting.

Taking my rifle with me, I eased my way over to the bunkhouse. Jim was coming around the corner of the bunkhouse, dripping wet and white-faced.

"I came out to see if you got the bear, Otis—and ran right into him," Jim said. "He took a swipe at me and knocked me down over the bank into the creek. That's closer'n I like to be to any bear."

No one felt much like sleeping for awhile so the boys came up to the cookhouse. I got my gas lantern going and we sat around and relived the adventure.

"You know, Otis, I wonder if you hit the bear at all. That shot you fired sounded more like it hit something steel outside," Andy said.

I laughed. "I *was* a little nervous, fellas. I probably hit an old barrel or something."

Next morning, Andy came over for breakfast grinning like crazy. "You know what you got last night, don't you?"

I flipped the pancakes on the griddle, then said, "No. Did I hit the bear?"

"Nope," Andy chuckled. "You got your cement mixer. There's a hole straight through it."

That wasn't the end of that saga, not the way stories travel around in the Bush. Everytime I went into McGrath, some fella'd ask me, "Well, Otis, you got that cement mixer dressed out yet?"

It was starting to get cold by late August. It'd freeze at night, which meant we couldn't sluice until the box thawed out—about 10 A.M. I reached Audrey by phone from McGrath on August 26. I was glad to hear she'd gone to a doctor and was getting good care. All of a sudden, I started thinking hard about going home.

We were a pretty ragged-looking bunch by early September. Myself, I'd lost about thirty pounds. The rest of the crew had lost weight, too. We looked tired and haggard.

"It's time to have a final cleanup, get our equipment stowed for the winter, and head for home, boys," I said. There sure wasn't any protest from them!

We picked up another 150 ounces of gold. David Strant stopped by and I told him we were about ready to leave. He said Shany West was bringing parts in for him, and he'd tell West to stop by and fly us to McGrath.

The next morning, I got up to fire the barrel stove at 4 A.M. and heard a noise. I stepped outside: sandhill cranes were passing over going south. Thousands of cranes. They were still flying over when daylight came.

On September 17, we took the radio down and got our gear in order. When we heard West's plane landing at Colorado Creek, we hiked up to our airstrip and waited. Well, we heard Shany West take off from the Strants' and keep going. So we walked back to camp, thinking he'd probably come the next day. He didn't. So we set the radio back up and got a message off to Ace Airway to come out. On September 22, Ace Airway flew in.

When we took off, I looked back at the camp. The aspens were yellow now and the hilltops were dusted with snow. Three moose were feeding in the valley. God, I hated to leave! I could feel my throat tighten up. I'd worked so hard and put so much of myself into that mine. I felt like I was abandoning that lonely-looking camp down below. As the plane headed for a pass in the Sunshine Mountains, I was feeling pretty low. Well, I'll call Audrey when I get to Anchorage and that'll give me a boost, I told myself.

When we landed in McGrath, I took old Jim's share of the take over to him.

"Sure glad to see you boys," he said. "I see you made it through your first year."

In the morning, we boarded a plane to Anchorage. When we got to the runway, lots of people had gathered to tell us good-bye. That surprised me. I shook hands and said we'd be seeing them next spring. We sold our gold in Anchorage. I settled up with the boys on their wages and paid off a few last bills we owed in Anchorage before boarding a plane for the Lower 48.

Altogether, I sold 270 ounces of gold that first year—

more than ninety thousand dollars' worth. Pretty good for our first year as gold miners.

But before I could leave, I had to get shots and papers for Dingo. I took him to a veterinarian's office.

"Yes, may I help you?" asked the receptionist.

"I need to get shots and papers on my Alaskan Dingo to take him to Minnesota with me," I told her.

"What breed of dog?" she asked, taking down my name and other information.

"Alaskan Dingo," I said. She nodded, wrote on her notepad, and told me to take a seat.

Five minutes later, I heard a male voice call out, "Send that man in with his Alaskan Dingo dog."

I went in and the vet was grinning ear to ear. "Well, Mr. Hahn, that's quite a fine Dingo you've got there," he said. "Looks like there's a fair amount of Norwegian elkhound and some Labrador blood in him, too."

I laughed and agreed. When Dingo and I were ready to leave, the vet said, "I'll bet you anything my receptionist is out there trying to look up Alaskan Dingo right now."

He would have won that bet. When I paid my bill, I saw a thick book with pictures of dogs open on her desk.

At the airport, I got Dingo crated up for the flight and settled into my airplane seat, ready for a long nap. But my mind kept thinking about things we'd do next spring—like building a different sluice box. Suddenly, crowding all of that out came a foreboding, a black cloud of doubt. What would I do about the White Wolf Mining Corporation board's lax performance? What had happened? Why didn't I receive minutes and reports as promised? Could I straighten all of that out? Was the chairman being purposely hard to reach?

I didn't have answers to any of those questions. Weary to the bone, I sat in my seat watching the sky turn from day to dusk to night.

CHAPTER 9

The Farm and the Board

"Dad, you look like a ghost of yourself! You're all bones," said my daughter Linda when I got off the plane.

My whole family—Audrey, my grown-up kids Linda, Terri, Randy, and Dave, their spouses, and a bunch of grandchildren—gave me the best airport welcome home I can remember. There was hand-shaking and hugging, some teary eyes, and feisty Dingo barking at us all.

We had a big family get-together in the yellow house on the farm at Mizpah, everyone talking lots. Audrey put the coffee pot on and set out cake and cookies and milk. We all sat up late. I met my baby granddaughter, Nicole, for the first time, found out what had been happening in their lives, and told them about our mining adventures.

"If Dingo's a bear dog, did he kill bears in Alaska, Grandpa?" my grandson Mike asked me.

"Not exactly," I said. "What he did was bark to warn us

that a bear was around. Then he'd run off or get under something and hide."

The kids made a big fuss over Dingo. And I had a brand-new story to tell them about that Dingo hound of mine. At the Minneapolis/St. Paul airport, I had to collect my luggage and Dingo to switch to the airplane that would take me to Bemidji, Minnesota. I took Dingo out of his cage and put him on a leash, and a porter helped me with the gear. I had to hand Dingo over to the man in charge of screening folks. I walked through the sensor and reclaimed Dingo. I thought the porter was taking me out to the gate, but instead, he delivered me to the security office. A man grabbed my suitcase, unzipped it, pulled out my pistol, and hollered for a guard. Several guards came over, along with a no-nonsense sergeant. In all the hubbub, Dingo ambled over to that sergeant, lifted his leg, and wet all over the man's uniformed leg and polished black boot.

"Get that wild dog out of here," shouted the sergeant.

A woman in charge of the security office came over. "What are you doing with this man in here?" she asked.

"He had this pistol in his luggage," said one of the guards.

"And look what his crazy dog did," bellowed the sergeant.

The woman eyed my large suitcase. "That's too big for a carry-on. Is that luggage you are checking through?"

"Yes. I was told to collect my luggage before I switched over to the Bemidji flight."

"Go get your luggage checked in and catch your plane. You're okay as long as you're not carrying that pistol on the airplane with you," she said.

I headed out of there pronto with Dingo and the porter toting my gear. The woman walked along with us down the hallway.

"You know, we ought to have more dogs come through here. It would keep a few egos in check," she laughed.

It was good to laugh and talk with my family. I was glad to be home.

The next morning, Dave and I walked around the farm. I matched my gait to his stride. Dave's taller than me, about six-foot-two, 190 pounds, with a mustache he's worn all of his adult years, big and capable hands, and a happy disposition. He's always loved farming.

It was fall harvest season. Due to scant rainfall, the pastures and grain fields looked rusty and burnt. As we walked, Dave brought me up to date on the farm situation. We had a lot of money into the place and lots of hogs. I'd sent Dave money when I could, after I found out that farmers were in bad shape that year.

When I'd left last spring, forty-pound hogs were up to sixty-five dollars. Now, prices had dropped down to eighteen dollars, and Dave calculated we had thirty-five dollars a head into our 150 brood sows. Even if we got that price, we wouldn't come out ahead.

"I've taken a job at Potlatch Company in Bemidji to make ends meet, Dad," Dave told me. That meant he had to drive back and forth five days a week. He'd found a young farm hand to hire economically, but Dave was under a lot of stress. "I just don't see how I'll make it if prices stay down," he worried.

"Well, try to hang in there another year," I counseled. "I'll help you out as much as I can."

I could tell Dave wondered if that was the right route to take. But the farm that had been my dad's farmstead was dear to me. The very lay of the land triggered memories of my youth. Dave went off to his job, but I lingered in the thirsty, parched fields.

I remembered my dad telling me stories when we worked together on rainy days mending machinery. One story was about haying out in a slough, some twenty miles from the home place. He and another cattle raiser went out to the big meadow sloughs twenty miles away and put up hay in the summer. Then they'd haul it home during the winter to feed the cattle.

At first, they made the forty-mile round-trip to haul hay in one day, but that was awfully hard. So they built a cabin to use for overnight shelter and put a stove in it, but when they got out there to work, some trapper'd stolen the stove.

"Well, Son, it was thirty below, so we just cut a bigger hole in the roof where the stovepipe had been and built a fire on the cabin's dirt floor. The next morning, we were coal black from the smoke and soot," Dad told me with a hearty chuckle. He put a lot of zest into living in this hard-to-farm northern Minnesota land.

Dad was born in Ohio, and my mom in Illinois. They met and married in Illinois. Dad was a little on the adventurous side: he wanted to come north to Minnesota. My grandfather, a minister in Ohio, died, so Grandma Hahn came north with my parents in 1919. Those first years, Dad drove horses for logging camps and worked on the railroad out of Black Duck. He bought 120 acres of this farm from a logging outfit and settled on it in 1925. He cleared 70 acres of it using a grub hoe and horses. When I took over the farm, Audrey and I bought more land: we farmed about 650 acres.

I once asked Dad why he bought this land with a slough running through it. He said, "Well, it was all stumps and big trees out here then. The slough was the only place we could get hay."

It was tough out here during the Depression, but Mom and Dad raised their four kids without taking a handout from anyone. Many mornings, a tramp would be sitting on the porch waiting for breakfast. Dad'd give him an ax and a saw, and have him cut and split wood until breakfast was ready. That's how he got lots of his wood for the year.

Dad was dark-complected, a short and stocky man with an even temper about most things. But there was one time when he wasn't even-tempered. They had a county fair at

Northome, and boxers and wrestlers would come and take on all comers. Dad was interested in watching the fights. One year, he bought a ticket and went in the tent. The wrestler who was taking tickets said, "Hey, you hay-picker, where'd you steal the ticket?"

My dad said, "I bought it a few minutes ago."

"You're a damn liar," said the wrestler.

Which was the wrong thing to say to Dad, who took pride in his honesty. Being a good, strapping man, he took on the wrestler. When it was all over, both the wrestler and a boxer were on the ground. Dad was still standing. He was a decent man, and lots of people respected him. So did I.

When I was a kid, we had to make our own fun. Mine was trapping: minks, weasels, some bobcats. The extra money I made selling pelts helped pay for our clothes. Sometimes I wonder how my mother managed. Dad would go off to work in lumber camps, and Mom took charge of milking and feeding the cattle, and the farm work plus running the household. She had to pump her own water, heat it on the stove, and wash clothes on a scrub board. Of course, all of us kids did our part. No doubt in our minds: chores and farmwork came first. If we had time left over, then we could do what we wanted.

Grandma Hahn lived with us and took charge of our religion. She got us to church and Sunday school. When I was little, she'd put me on a sled and pull me the mile or so to the church. She also made certain that we got to Bible camp every summer. Grandma Hahn died in 1939 and called each one of us into her room to say good-bye before she closed her eyes for good.

The old farm place held lots of memories for me. I hated to think of losing it. That winter, I stayed busy. Farm machinery and buildings needed repairs. Audrey and I did the livestock chores and everything we could to help Dave out. I also fattened up on Audrey's pot roasts, mashed potatoes and gravy, chocolate cake, and apple pie. Audrey had a birdfeeder by the house and around the first of January, she told me she had a surprise for me. At the feeder were small gray birds with a red stripe over the eye—redpolls. We saw lots of those little birds up at Bear Creek, their summer habitat.

All did not go without mishap, though. One morning, Dave and I were trying to put a big sow into a farrowing pen. She wasn't buying the idea and headed off down the hog house alley. Audrey came around the corner—to see that sow heading straight at her. Audrey jumped up in the air and came down straddling the sow's back. She rode the sow backwards a ways, then toppled off. Well, I'm afraid Dave and I both laughed. Audrey was mad as heck. She definitely wasn't amused. And it turned out not to be funny: she'd broken her arm.

Weeks and months whizzed by. I contacted some of the board members, but it was hard to come up with a meeting date that suited the majority of us. At last, I set a time and date and scheduled a White Wolf Mining board meeting. By then, it was March.

It turned out that almost all the investors—mostly doctors and attorneys—would be attending, a few even coming up from Arizona. A couple of nights before the meeting, a doctor who was an investor called me. "Just what are the problems we'll be discussing?" he asked.

"Well, the corporation gave me very little backing all summer," I told him. "There were committees that were supposed to be carrying out duties including setting up a bank account in Anchorage. Those things didn't get done."

With Audrey's help, I wrote a formal letter stating my position and the complaints I had. In the letter, I detailed specifics including the failure of White Wolf Mining officers to cancel the insurance on the truck after I notified them by telephone that I'd sold it (which cost us an $830 refund), and their failure to mail monthly financial statements (only two were received all summer). I specifically wanted to know why the officers hadn't followed through on things they said they would do.

That letter was read at the March 10 meeting in International Falls and responded to by the chairman and others. Then I stood up and told the investors how I saw the situation. I stated that I could no longer be president of the corporation if it continued to operate in this fashion. The doctor who'd called me said, "I think we've put too much of a burden on Otis. Running the mining operation is a full-time job. How about if you just do that, Otis, as the general manager, and let someone else serve as president?"

I wholeheartedly agreed. "Well, who would you recommend to be president then?" was his next question.

I thought about that. "How about Gene Bradley?" I answered. "He's been out to see the operation in person." That's who the board voted in.

In addition, the chairman stepped down and the board picked a different investor for that position, too.

I didn't have much stomach for any of this. The past chairman and I simply didn't see things the same way. After the meeting, he drafted a letter that was mailed to all investors including myself. In it, he contended that I'd exaggerated or misinterpreted his actions or lack of action, and that some of my accusations were false. Maybe it looked that way to him; but deep within my heart, I knew that the things I brought to the investors' attention were true. There were hard feelings between us, which I sincerely regretted. After all, he'd been largely responsible for recruiting the mine's initial investors. I just hoped that the coming mining season would see more communication between myself and the board, and a better grasp on their part of the financial workings of an Alaska-based mining operation.

During the meeting, I'd shown them slides I'd taken at the mine. It was a good way to acquaint them with the operation and to point out the need for new dragline parts. They'd been enthusiastic and put up an extra ten thousand to get the dragline working properly. After the meeting, we mingled and talked. One investor from Arizona came up to me and said, "We know what your trouble is, Otis. I hope what we did tonight will eliminate a lot of your difficulties. I want you to know that I believe in what you are doing. I think you are going to succeed in this mine."

That made me feel good. With grievances aired and a change in officers, I was feeling optimistic.

As the new mining season approached, I bought another dragline in Minnesota. I disassembled it and took all the good parts off of it to use in rebuilding our dragline at Bear Creek. We had to transport the parts from Minnesota to Anchorage and fly them in to McGrath and out to the mine. I wanted to get that done in March before the airstrip turned to spring-thaw mush. So I sent Andy ahead to meet up with Shany West and oversee flying the parts and groceries into the camp. When he left, I called my grocery supplier and placed about a five-thousand-dollar order to be delivered to McGrath.

Before I left, Dave and I took another walk around the farm. A flock of geese flew over headed north.

"Dad, you'll have to hurry to beat them up to Alaska," Dave said. "Oh, I'll beat them, all right," I smiled. "They'll be stopping to feed and rest along the way."

We went through the gate off the county road and into the field.

"Do you remember who's buried on that side of the gate, Dave?"

"Yep. Kelly, your old German shepherd. And Tina, Mom's little Pomeranian, is buried on the other side of the gate."

Out in that field stood one big, old elm tree. We headed toward it.

"Your grandpa, aunts, and uncles and myself ate many a lunch under that old elm," I said. "Dad left it there so we'd have shade when we were out here haying and working.

Your grandma always brought lunch out to us, and we'd sit beneath the tree to eat."

"You and I and the rest of us kids ate lots of lunches under that elm, too," Dave said. "But you know, Dad, the tree is dying."

I nodded and patted the rough bark. "Yes. It looks like it's got Dutch Elm disease. Pretty soon, the old tree will be gone. That's the way life is. Over the years, things change."

"Things haven't changed for the better for farmers around here this winter," Dave said. "The price of hogs has gotten even worse."

We headed back toward the gate. I had to clear my throat before I could talk. "I know, Dave. It really doesn't look good. If I were you, I think I'd keep fifty of my best brood sows and sell the rest. Plant maybe twenty acres of corn. If hog prices are still bad next fall, well, we'll just have to do the best we can. I've got a mortgage on the machinery, and the way prices are now, we can't even afford to keep up the equipment."

Dave and I didn't look at each other. We were both feeling pretty sad. We just walked through that field, side by side.

I notified my crew that it'd soon be time to head up north. Tim and Brent were coming out again, but Jim wouldn't be working this season. I hired a couple more Minnesota fellows: Frank Conway, a muscular man in his mid-twenties, a good equipment operator; and Jeff Truman, a tall, slender, quiet guy, a mechanic and welder who also operated heavy machinery. I wanted another mechanic around as a backup, in case something went awry with Andy.

"Are you up to cooking for us this season?" I asked Audrey. She nodded and said, "It's no picnic, Otis, but I don't want to stay here all summer without you. I'll be ready to leave for Alaska when you are ready for me to come out."

A few weeks passed, and I got uneasy. Andy hadn't called to report on his progress. Finally, I called a friend in

McGrath to find out if Andy had gotten the parts and groceries out to the camp.

"Well, Otis, not much is happening," he said. "Your parts are in McGrath but nothing's been hauled out to the mine. I hear Shany West and Andy have been kicking up their heels a bit in Anchorage."

Right away, I called my supplier in Anchorage and canceled the grocery order. I didn't want my whole season's worth of food supplies sitting on the runway in McGrath and freezing!

"Maybe I should be upset, Audrey, but it sort of seems like a fitting start to mining season number two," I said when I hung up the phone. "I've just gotten a big reminder that nothing is predictable when it comes to gold mining."

"Well, Otis, I guess that's part of the adventure," Audrey teased.

I sighed. "Yep. And if we want to mine this season, I'd better get myself up to Alaska right now."

CAMP SITE
Cook House, Meat House, Bunk House and Tool Shed

Otis, Audrey and their dog, Dingo, 1500 feet above the cook house.

Inside of cook house.

LEFT: Eskimo girl sitting between mammoth tusks.

BOTTOM: Mammoth tusk and skull.

TOP: Dragline under ice.

LEFT: Load of machinery north to Alaska somewhere in the Yukon.

Tractor fell through ice.

Trail from McGrath to the mine - 110 miles.

TOP:
Mining area.

MIDDLE:
Sluice box
in operation.

BOTTOM:
Gold in
sluice box.

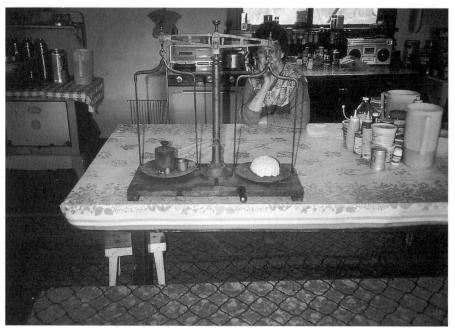

Audrey weighing 130 ounces with a gold ingot scale.

TOP: A worried D8 Cat driver crossing a one mile wide river.

LEFT: Otis and Audrey in the airport lobby waiting for air plane.

C119 delivering supplies for the summer.

LEFT: Beaver air plane.

RIGHT: Runway for D119 that brought in the summer supplies.

TOP: Barber shop
open once a month.

LEFT: A bad flood.

CHAPTER 10

Wings

On April 1, I arrived in McGrath. When the plane leveled off to land, my fears were confirmed. Stacks of our dragline parts were piled up alongside the runway.

A group of about thirty people had come to watch us land, but Andy and Shany West weren't around. I recognized most of the folks and spent some time shaking hands. A young Native boy in the crowd grinned at me and yelled, "Are you going hunting for cement mixers this summer, Mr. Hahn?"

It looked like Andy and Shany West had made maybe two trips out to the mine. Three-fourths of the parts were still in McGrath. Well, I wasn't about to wait around for the two of them to show up.

Frank and Jeff, my new crew members, were with me. Audrey, Tim, and Brent would come up later when we had the camp opened up. With all the gear we had to bring, Frank, Jeff, Dingo, and I had driven to Anchorage in a van. We'd left our van there when we flew to McGrath. Now we

83

wouldn't have to take cabs everywhere when we were in Anchorage to buy supplies and sell gold.

I left the boys and Dingo in McGrath, caught a flight back to Anchorage, and located another airplane—a Beaver on skis—and hired the pilot to fly in the parts and groceries. Then I backtracked to McGrath. When I went in to talk to Ace Airway about flying us out to the mine, I found out that the pilot I'd often used before was gone.

"He left Anchorage with a plane last Christmas and hasn't been seen since," said the Ace Airway manager. "I figure he went down in hundred-mile-per-hour winds over the Alaska Range."

The fellow was matter-of-fact about it: that's part of life in the Bush. I arranged to have Ace Airway drop the boys and me and the dog off at the mine.

The airplane passed over the snow-topped Sunshine Mountains and the foothills deep green with spruce, nosed into the valley, and put down on our little airstrip. Dingo nearly went crazy sniffing around, then bounded off down the trail. Damn, but I was glad to be back, and so was he.

The battered collection of tin-sided buildings—the old cookshack on skids, the screened meat cache, the bunkhouse and sheds—sat there, waiting for us. The Cat and loader got through the winter just fine. I sent the boys off to unpack and get the bunkhouse in order while I got settled in the cookhouse.

I saw a couple of little redpolls perched on a woodpile. I may have beaten the geese back to Alaska, but the redpolls got here before me.

A few days later, Andy and Shany West flew in. I met them on the trail to the camp. "West, you're out of a job," I told him. "I've heard that the two of you have been having a big time in Anchorage."

"Otis, we had lots of bad weather for flying," Andy said.

"Maybe so," I said, "but I sure would feel a lot better about things if you'd called to let me know."

Andy stood there, fingering that beard of his.

"I've hired another pilot to bring in the parts," I said. "Now, we've got a fresh mining season ahead of us. There's lots to be done, Andy. After you stow your gear in the bunkhouse, you can give the front-end loader a good going over."

That ended the discussion. Andy headed for the bunkhouse and Shany West walked back to the airstrip. I did some odd jobs around camp, fiddled around with the old light plant, got the radio set up, and waited for the Beaver—and waited and waited—a couple of weeks. Meanwhile it warmed up a bit, which made me nervous. The runway was starting to get sloppy.

Finally, I heard the Beaver coming in. The pilot landed okay with the first load. But when he brought in the second load, the plane put down on the runway and started to slide. I watched, helpless, sweating like crazy. The Beaver corrected, then slid to the other side of the runway, and stopped just short of veering off into the trees.

"That landing stood my hair on end," I said when the pilot got out of the plane.

"I didn't much care for it either," he said. After the freight was unloaded, I told him, "You might as well go back to Anchorage. I'll have to come up with some other plan for getting the rest of the parts in. The runway's too soft and slushy right now for you to fly in again."

If I had my own airplane and a dependable pilot, I could have avoided the mess I'm in now, I thought. We need our own airplane! Considering the problems we'd had last year with air transportation and the way things were starting out this year, having our own wings appealed to me. Maybe we could swing it.

By asking a few questions in McGrath, I found out that Shany West had purchased a Beaver airplane from a fellow in Anchorage last winter but failed to make the payments on it. The fellow had taken it back.

"What do you think about buying a used airplane of our own?" I asked the White Wolf Mining president by telephone from McGrath, after I explained our predicament. I told him

I had a lead on a used Beaver. He said he'd discuss it with the board. When I called back later, he said the board agreed that we needed an airplane of our own to fly in supplies and for emergencies.

"Go take a look at the plane and find out the price and then report back to us," he said.

I went to Anchorage and found the white-with-red-trim Beaver. It was the kind of plane we needed, with a 150-gallon fuel tank on it. Winton Henry, the owner, said, "Well, West was pretty hard on that plane over the winter. I'd agree to completely go over the engine and fix anything that needs fixing and have it okayed by the airplane inspectors here. My price for the Beaver is forty-five thousand dollars, which includes wheels and skis."

I called my White Wolf Mining contact. "Go ahead, Otis. Buy the airplane," he said. "If you can arrange financing through a bank in Anchorage, that'd be best."

I agreed with him. We'd done our financing before through a bank in International Falls, but it made a lot more sense to me to use a bank in Alaska since that's where we were operating our mine.

Winton Henry took me to the bank where he does business. The banker and I talked. "We'd be happy to finance the airplane, Otis," he said. "But I want you to have your company send me a financial report. I need to look at that to see if you have enough equity in the operation and check out the figures before I can issue a loan."

I phoned my White Wolf Mining contact right away. "A financial report needs to be mailed to the banker immediately," I said. I gave him the banker's name and bank address.

Before I left Anchorage, Winton Henry said he'd get the airplane in top condition as soon as possible. "Do you want me to bring it to McGrath for you or do you have a pilot who can fly it there from Anchorage?" he asked.

"No, I don't have a pilot, but I'm sure in the market for one," I replied. "I need someone who can fly the plane and work on the mining crew, too, since I don't have enough flying for full-time. But there's plenty of mechanical work and lots of bookkeeping that needs to be done. Do you know anyone who might be interested?"

"Well, I'll keep my eye out for a pilot looking for that kind of work," Henry said.

A couple of weeks later, I called him. He said he'd found a pilot, but "I've had a little trouble with the engine," he allowed. "We got the Beaver overhauled and I took it out over the bay to try it out. Otis, the engine blew up. Something must've happened in the overhaul. I was lucky to be able to land it on a dirt runway along the bay. I've ordered a brand-new engine, but it'll be another week or two before I get it in."

A "little trouble" indeed!

The delay left me in a bad spot. Tim, Brent, and Audrey had flown into camp by then. We should have been overhauling the dragline—but most of my parts were still on the runway in McGrath. So I put the boys to work cutting wood and doing lots of odd jobs around the camp.

"Am I ever glad you got my running water hooked up," Audrey told Tim. By the cookhouse was a stack of six fifty-five-gallon barrels, ends cut off except for the bottom one, all welded together. A small pump filled the barrels from Cripple Creek, which ran behind the cookhouse. Tim had tinkered with the outfit and got it working. No more carrying water from the creek to do dishes!

One night Audrey and I walked up into the cut where we'd worked last year.

"Look, Otis," she said, pointing at a clump of scrub trees. "Those two ravens are back. The old Natives say when someone dies their spirit returns as a raven. Do you believe that?"

"A few years ago, I'd have said no," I said. I watched the huge black birds eyeing us and thought about how two of old Jim's sons died out here. "Now, I'm not so sure."

I called Winton Henry a week or so later. "The plane is ready to go," he said. "I think you should fly in and meet the pilot. He's been working on the plane, getting it ready."

I hopped a plane to Anchorage and met Tommy Tolman, a slightly built, good-looking fellow with a likeable manner. The Beaver looked great. And White Wolf Mining was painted on the tail in black letters. The airplane was really ours! Tommy and I headed for the Bear Creek mine, bringing a load of supplies from Anchorage with us.

Tommy sat easy at the controls until we neared Bear Creek. I was in the co-pilot's seat. When we took a preliminary pass over the airstrip, Tommy's face and body tensed up. "That's a tricky airstrip to land on with a full load," he said, glancing at me. "I've never landed on such a short runway before." (Our runway measured about thirteen hundred feet, but only nine hundred feet of it were usable at that time.)

It seemed to me that Tommy was coming in way too fast. I felt sweat trickle down my face. "Watch it, Tommy! You're coming in way too hot," I yelled. "Go around and come back again." He shot me a look that told me I'd stepped on his toes and he didn't like it, but he did pass over the runway. The next time around, he cut down on the speed and we made a good landing.

After we were on the ground, Tommy asked, "Is there another runway around here?"

"There's Folger Field, but it hasn't been used since last year. The best airstrip is Strant's runway over at Colorado Creek. It's a half-mile in length and in good condition."

"How about if I fly the dragline parts into the strip at Colorado Creek?" Tommy asked. "I'd rather do that since I don't know this airplane all that well, yet."

The idea didn't thrill me. That meant I'd have to use my Cat to haul the supplies all the way from Colorado Creek into our Bear Creek camp. But I decided I'd better go along with what the pilot wanted.

Tommy flew the first several loads of our dragline parts to the Colorado Creek airstrip. Then, Tommy called me on the radio. "Otis, I'm going to fly in empty and land at Bear Creek tonight and see how it goes," he said. He did—and that red-and-white Beaver set down nice and smooth. Lucky for us, thawing had slowed down, and the airstrip was still usable.

"I'll bring the rest of the loads in here, Otis," Tommy told me in the morning, which sure made things easier for me.

As it turned out, we had to make another trip into Anchorage for extra parts, so I invited Audrey to come along. As we neared the international airport, I heard Tommy call the tower to get permission and clearance to land. Suddenly, the plane veered off in a radical turn to the east.

"We've lost contact with the radio tower—our radio's out—and we've got to get the hell out of here," Tommy said. "There are 747s coming in and out. I don't dare land without approval."

"So where do we land?"

"I remember an old dirt strip east of town. It's not great but I think we can land on it," he said.

We bumped down on the dirt strip and came to a stop just fifty feet short of going into the woods.

"You and Audrey wait here," Tommy said. "I'll walk down the road to a house and try to phone a buddy of mine to pick us up."

An hour and a half later Tommy and his buddy drove up. Tommy looked pretty pale.

"I think we're in trouble," he said, as soon as Audrey and I climbed into the car. "I just heard on the car radio that a small plane went down in the inlet. There are two air rescue helicopters and two small planes out there searching for us, Otis! I've got to call the air control people as soon as we get into town."

We stopped at a phone booth and Tommy called. "They want to see me right away at the tower," he said. So we drove to the airport and Tommy went in.

He was in there for nearly an hour and came out shaking his head. "Boy, did they ever overhaul me. They wanted to know why we didn't call in sooner and said it costs a lot to have search planes go out, plus they had to hold up air traffic over the inlet while the search was going on. They aren't happy with us."

"I'm just glad we *aren't* down in that inlet," I said. "We'll get the radio fixed in the morning."

"I told them we couldn't do anything but what we did," Tommy said. "They told me to bring the plane in tomorrow. They're going to check it over before we leave Anchorage."

We did as they asked. Mid-morning on our way back to camp, Audrey said, "And I thought this was going to be an uneventful trip."

By May 18, summer was coming on. The creeks were running wide open, and things had thawed out. That spring, we'd gotten in the habit of listening to our radio in the cookshack in the evening. And Audrey would keep it on for company during the day.

McGrath's Bush radio station is a little like rural party telephone lines, everybody listening in and knowing your business. You hear everything on Bush radio—from personal birthday greetings, to announcements that relatives are coming out for a visit, to notification by your mechanic that broken-down machinery has been repaired.

We were listening to the radio one evening when the announcer dedicated a Johnny Cash song, "I Walk the Line," "to Audrey and the boys out on Bear Creek."

"Come on over to the station when you're in town and let us know what's going on out there," the guy said. Audrey got a kick out of it. "I wonder who made that request?" she said. We still don't know.

One morning, a Bush radio message came for me from Mr. Henry in Anchorage. He wanted me to call him right away.

When I last saw Henry in Anchorage, I thought I had everything squared away regarding the purchase of the Beaver. Why was Winton Henry contacting me?

CHAPTER 11

The Mammoth Find

Given the temperamental nature of our radio-phone, placing a call to Anchorage or anyplace else was never a certain thing. But luck was with me: I managed to contact Winton Henry from the camp.

"Otis, I need to talk to you because the bank didn't hear from your mining corporation officers back in Minnesota," said Henry. "What do you plan to do about paying for the airplane?"

My stomach tightened, but I kept my voice calm. I didn't want Winton Henry to know how much this turn of events disturbed me. "I thought everything was being taken care of," I told him. "I'll have to contact my White Wolf Mining partners back in Minnesota. It might take me a couple of days, but I'll let you know as soon as I talk to them."

I tried to reach International Falls on my radio, but I couldn't get the call through. The next day I flew to McGrath and called from the pay phone in the bar.

"The board has decided to finance the airplane in International Falls, but we just haven't gotten around to doing it yet," the new director said.

"Well, I wish someone had bothered to let me know. What kind of interest will you be paying there?" I asked.

"Fourteen percent," he said.

"That really doesn't make sense to me when we could finance it here in Anchorage for nine percent," I said, "but if that's what you've decided, fine. Just do it quickly because the man who sold us the Beaver wants to be paid."

Before I left McGrath, I called Winton Henry back. "My partners have decided to finance the airplane back in International Falls," I told him. "You'll be getting paid as soon as the loan goes through."

Tommy flew me back out to the camp. There wasn't much conversation. My mind kept dwelling on the telephone call to International Falls. I surely did have some misgivings about the financing of the airplane. I hoped my partners would get the financing squared away. It didn't set well with me to be putting Mr. Henry off just because they hadn't gotten around to taking care of arranging for a loan.

Meanwhile we worked at getting our dragline set up so we'd be ready to sluice. One morning, Audrey and I were in the cookhouse bedroom, about ready to get up and start our day, when a terrific crash shook the little cookshack.

I jumped up quick and grabbed my rifle. "Whatever is out there must be awfully big, Audrey!"

I opened the bedroom door. Partway through the cookhouse kitchen window was a very determined 350-pound black bear. He'd broken the window and was clawing at everything he possibly could. The crash we heard was the top of the cookstove, which he'd torn off and knocked to the floor.

I fired. The force of the bullet drove him back out the window. Audrey stood there, shaking her head. Shredded curtains, cooking pots, canisters, and parts of the stove littered the floor.

"He surely did manage to do a lot of damage," Audrey said. We stepped outside into drizzly rain. The bear lay dead on a bank by the cookhouse. Dingo started sniffing at the bear when the carcass shifted suddenly. That little dog leaped straight up in the air and took off for the cookhouse door.

"Look at those claws!" Audrey said. "I wouldn't want to be slapped with those!"

Audrey got some breakfast fixed in spite of the mess and packed up our lunches. We left the bear at the edge of the campground to bury that night.

When Audrey wrote a letter back to our kids in Minnesota that week, she told them about the bear in the cookhouse kitchen. "And I told them to tell the grandkids that Grandpa shot a bear in his underwear," she grinned.

In the next few days, I noticed that our dogs hadn't left camp. That was odd: usually, they'd be out rabbit hunting every morning. I figured that wolves must be around pretty close to the camp. I also hadn't seen "our" old cow moose: she'd shown up that spring when we got to camp and had been hanging around. We'd see her nearly every day.

"Otis, do you hear something outside?" Audrey asked one night after we'd gone to bed. I got up and looked out. Not far from the cookhouse stood the cow moose nursing a pair of twin calves. They looked to be three or four days old. Audrey and I watched until the trio moved away from the camp site. I thought about those calves that night as I fell asleep and also about the wolves we'd encountered out here. Predator and prey, life and death. It was all part of nature's cycle.

We kept getting ground ready to sluice. One noon, Tim came running into camp short of breath. "Otis! Audrey! You won't believe this," he yelled. "Follow me. Have I got something to show you."

It had been a long morning. I was tired and glad that we were working close enough to camp to come into the cookhouse for lunch. "This better be spectacular, Tim," I grumbled, reluctant to leave the hot coffee and sandwiches made from Audrey's crusty wheat bread.

Tim, Audrey, and I tramped through scrub spruce and tundra and moss up to the ground Tim had been stripping. Sun glinted on something white in a pile of earth that had been bulldozed by the Cat.

"Mammoth bones!" Tim exclaimed. "Those are leg bones. I've uncovered some vertebrae, and I hope we'll dig up some tusks, too."

When we went back to the cookhouse for lunch, Tim told the rest of the crew about the bones. The mammoth find generated lots of lunch break conversation. "I've heard that ivory tusks are worth a lot," said Brent. "We'll probably find ivory up there, don't you think, Otis?"

"It's pretty likely," I said, helping myself to a plump, raisin-filled oatmeal cookie. "I tell you what, boys. If we find ivory, we'll locate a buyer and split the pay evenly among us. This doesn't relate directly to what we're here to do—gold mining. So, just consider any ivory we find a bonus. Does that sound fair to you?"

They all liked that idea. It seemed a fair way to deal with what might have become a sticky issue: the possibility of a "finders keepers" attitude.

Stripping continued. A few days later, Tim said, "I think we've found a tusk!"

Sure enough, sunk down in the gravel was the end of an ivory tusk. Tim power-washed that spot and got the gravel and dirt off. The uncovered tusk measured ten feet six from tip to tip and the butt end was eight inches in diameter.

"Wow. I never dreamed we'd be mining mammoth bones and tusks along with gold out here," said my crewman Jeff.

It took a stretch of imagination to believe that hairy mammoths lived here once. But the evidence lay all around us. As it turned out, Tim knew a little something about bones and animal relics. When the workday was done, he'd carefully bring the bones and ivory we'd found into camp.

By the time we started sluicing, around the tenth or so of July, we'd made other discoveries, including the remains of twin calves and a female mammoth carrying yet another calf. In all, we'd found seven large tusks and some smaller broken-up pieces of ivory.

One evening, when Audrey went out to collect bones with Tim, she picked up a tooth she saw on the ground. It looked like a gigantic bear tooth to me.

"I think that might be quite rare," guessed Tim.

Around ten that night, we heard a small plane approaching. I went out to look: it was David Strant in his little Super Cub. He pulled back the throttle and set down on our airstrip.

Audrey put the coffeepot on; David and Craig Allen came walking into camp a bit later. They were hoping we had some tractor parts they needed. Audrey poured cups of coffee and set out plates of pineapple upside-down cake.

"Say, I noticed some ivory tusks on our way into camp," said Craig.

"Yes, we've found quite a few," I said.

"Did you know that we have people from the University of Alaska over at Colorado Creek?" he asked. I shook my head.

"We have a find of three big tusks," Craig continued. "They aren't all thawed out of the bank yet, but it looks like one skull is still attached to a pair of tusks. The university people—a man and his wife and a younger fellow—think they might be able to recover all the bones of that mammoth. They're camped out in a tent, so we invite them up for meals now and then."

"I wouldn't mind talking to them about our find," I said.

David said, "They'd probably like that. The older fellow's spent his whole life examining these finds. Some of your tusks are in good condition. I found out that a year ago, an eleven-foot tusk in McGrath sold for a thousand dollars a foot."

I arranged with David to invite the people over to our camp for dinner the next night. Tommy'd be there to pick them up around 5 P.M.

Audrey told Craig she hoped his wife, Fran, could come along. "We can catch up with one another and it'd be nice to have another pair of hands to help with the dinner."

Audrey was up hustling around early in the morning. "Otis, you've got a gift bottle of wine stowed under your bed. Why don't you chill that for our guests tonight?" she said.

I chuckled. "Well, I'll do that, Audrey. I'll bring in some glacier ice today to put in a bucket with the wine. It'll be a real uptown deal here tonight."

That afternoon, good-natured Fran trotted into camp ahead of the guests, gave Audrey a big hug, and pitched in helping get the meal on the table.

Tim hurried up to the airstrip and walked back to camp with the experts, talking about bones and tusks all the way. Our guests turned out to be jovial people.

Audrey outdid herself: the aroma of beef roasting called us all to the cookhouse. She'd made mashed potatoes, gravy, and corn, and had even set jars of wildflowers on the table. It reminded me of home.

That night we stayed out until one in the morning looking at tusks and bones with our guests. There was no trouble seeing because it was still daylight. Tim showed them the bones and tusks he'd collected.

"You've got a short-faced bear tooth," the expert said, studying the tooth that Audrey found. "That bear very likely weighed over three thousand pounds. And you've got teeth from some 250-pound beavers."

The university experts also identified a small horse tooth, but there were many bones they were unable to identify. Tim asked the older gentleman about the Colorado Creek dig.

"Well, it's going very slowly," he said. "We've been there three weeks now. Every day, as it thaws, we go out and carefully brush the debris off the bones. We were hoping to find an entire mammoth skeleton to take to the university and assemble, but now I doubt that we'll find the complete skeleton."

Before they left, the older man gave me an envelope containing a tuft of mammoth hair, which I in turn gave to Tim. It was a memorable evening for all of us at the camp.

We didn't see the university experts again. They left Colorado Creek before the summer ended without finding the whole mammoth skeleton. They did take the skull with attached tusks, though, and I've since talked to people who've seen it displayed in a glass case at the university.

It was 2 A.M. before I got to bed. When I fell asleep, bears and mammoths—gigantic prehistoric beasts—lumbered through my dreams, along with gangly moose calves sniffing at a boulder-size, shiny gold ingot in front of the cookhouse door.

CHAPTER 12

Paying the Bills

Tommy had been flying fuel to the mining camp nearly every day. On one trip, he passed over the airstrip and kept right on going. I wondered what was up. Pretty soon, Audrey came tearing out to me. Tommy had radioed her in the kitchen.

"You've got to get up to the airstrip right away," Audrey said. "The cow moose and her twin calves are lying down on the runway and Tommy can't land."

I dropped what I was doing and took off, knowing Tommy wouldn't consider it a lark flying around with 150 gallons of fuel in the tank, waiting for the moose family to move on.

I was more than satisfied with Tommy: he'd turned out to be a good pilot, a hard worker, and a good bookkeeper. As soon as I hired Tommy, I'd shifted the bookkeeping and correspondence chores over to him. Deep down, I was relieved not to have to depend on Andy to do my writing and my books.

We were sluicing and putting in long hours—and once

again, I was faced with no communication from the White Wolf Mining officers, and no clue about our finances. I couldn't afford to take time out to fly into McGrath to contact my White Wolf Mining Corporation officers, but on many of Tommy's trips to McGrath, I had him call International Falls to see if they'd put money in our account. All Tommy got was the run-around.

Finally, one of the boys came up to me and said, "Otis, the crew needs to be paid. We've got car payments to meet and other bills to pay, too."

The next day, I told Tommy, "Today, when you fly into McGrath for fuel, I want you to call the White Wolf Mining treasurer and ask if there's enough money in the account to meet a payroll of around fifteen thousand dollars."

I was in the cookhouse when he returned. He came down first thing to report to me. "When I called your treasurer's office, he was busy on the phone and couldn't talk to me then, but his secretary said to call back in an hour. So I did. Your treasurer said he didn't have money in the account now, and it would take about a week for him to get money into an account in Anchorage for you."

I thanked Tommy, and he went out to unload the fuel. "Goddamn those guys back there!" I said to Audrey. I was boiling inside. "Damn! Damn! Damn! I wonder how they'd like it if I said, 'Tomorrow the boys are coming home because they won't work for no pay. What do you want to do? Close up the camp in the middle of summer? Let me see you make a decision on this.'"

I slammed the cookhouse screen door behind me and tackled a repair to the sluice box platform with a vengeance, hammering nails into boards and talking to myself.

"If we have a cleanup, and we get as much pay as I think is in this cut, then I'll sell the gold and I won't deposit it in the International Falls account. Instead, I'll pay off the Native corporation fuel bill in McGrath and the other bills, and pay my crew with the money from the gold sale." I hammered those nails hard. "Yes, that's what I'll do. And if there's money left over," *Whack, Whack, Whack,* "that can go into the International Falls account."

I felt a lot better by the time I got the sluice box platform fixed. That night when we had coffee at the long, wooden cookhouse table Audrey'd dressed up with flowered oilcloth, I told the crew we'd start a cleanup the next day.

"Then, I'll go into Anchorage with the gold, and all of you will be paid."

The next morning we started cleaning up. The gold looked good. In gold-mining tradition, we made bets on the amount of gold in the box. Everybody threw in ten dollars; the winner would get the pot. I'd kept close track of the hours that went into the sluice box, and figured the take would be at least 150 ounces. It took twelve hours to do the cleanup and get the gold into a marketable state. Andy retorted the gold that night so Audrey and I could leave for Anchorage in the morning. It turned out that Audrey won the pot with her guess of 167 ounces. We ended up with close to 170 ounces of gold.

That night, the boys made a long list of bank drafts and deposits for us to send when we cashed in the gold and they got paid. They also had a list of things they needed. In the morning, Audrey put the lists in her purse. "Do you think you are doing the right thing, Otis?" she asked as we got ready to leave.

"I'm doing the only damn thing I know to do," I said. "The crew is going to be paid today."

Tommy flew us to McGrath, and we took a commercial flight to Anchorage. I didn't want to leave the boys without a plane. Well, it turned out our flight was delayed by bad weather, so we didn't get into Anchorage until late Friday afternoon—too late to go to the smelter.

"It looks like we've got 170 ounces of gold to babysit until the smelter opens Monday morning," I told Audrey. I hadn't brought my briefcase, so we put the gold in Audrey's purse and went to a motel close to the airport.

"Maybe we could put the gold in the motel safe," Audrey suggested.

I shook my head. "Don't you remember hearing about the couple who came into Fairbanks last summer and did that? The safe was robbed that night, and they lost 300 ounces of gold. We'll just keep the gold with us."

I took a hot shower as soon as we got in. Then it was Audrey's turn for an hour-long soak in the tub. I ordered a bottle of wine from room service, poured a glass for Audrey, and took it in to her while she was in the tub.

"Not many mining camp cooks get this kind of treatment," I said.

Audrey took a sip of the wine and leaned back in the tub. "This camp cook's sure not complaining," she smiled. While we watched television that night, Audrey turned to me and said, "We should do this more often, Otis."

"From now on out, we will," I said.

We got a good night's sleep in a comfortable bed. Around noon the next day, we went out to shop around, but it didn't last very long. The gold was too heavy. I ended up carrying Audrey's purse awhile, but we headed back to the motel pretty fast. We spent the rest of the weekend sticking close to the motel.

On Monday morning, we went directly to the smelter. The gold brought close to eighty thousand dollars. I took the check from the smelter directly to the bank, and Audrey and I wrote out checks and deposits to mail for the boys. After that, I paid our Anchorage grocer.

Then I found a pay phone and called a White Wolf Mining board investor.

"I just sold the gold from our first cleanup," I told him.

"What did we make?" he asked.

"About eighty thousand dollars," I said. "But I want the board to know that I'm using most of that money to pay the bills we owe here and to pay my help. I figure there'll be about thirty thousand dollars left after that, which I'll deposit in the International Falls account."

There was a pause. "You know we set up a gold committee, and they decided you were to call us before you cashed in the gold," the fellow said. "Then they'd let you know what we decided to do."

"Well, that's the way it's supposed to work," I answered, my temper rising. "Only no one gets around to paying the bills. So I decided what to do and I did it. I paid the crew and I'm paying the bills. I can't operate on investors talking about what they are going to do and then doing nothing."

The fellow could tell I was upset. "Well, I guess what you did was the best thing to do under the circumstances," he said.

"You're damn right it's the best thing to do," I said. "Or else next week, you'd have a mining crew sitting on your porch in International Falls and a mining operation that'd be dead in Alaska."

Audrey leaned over my shoulder, put her hand on my arm, and said, "That's enough, Otis. Get off the phone."

My blood was boiling. I could hardly stop talking, but I knew Audrey was right.

I said, "You can report this to the board at your next meeting and send me a copy of the minutes with discussion of this matter," and I hung up the phone.

Based on past experience, I had a pretty slight chance of ever seeing any minutes at all. Sweat was running down my neck. I darn well knew that I'd be stepping on some toes by taking this course of action. But at that moment, I didn't care. I'd tried to be patient and cooperative and include the White Wolf Mining investors in my decisions, but that had gotten me nowhere.

At noon, we went back to the motel and put a call through to the Bear Creek radio-phone. I figured someone might be in the cookhouse fixing lunch, but I wasn't at all sure we'd get through on our temperamental camp phone. Then I heard Tommy's voice say, "This is Bear Creek. Go ahead."

I told him to tell the crew that they'd all been paid. "Wahoo! That's good news," he said. "We're doing fine out here. Jeff and Andy and Frank got the sluice box moved, so everything's ready to go."

"Tell them to go ahead and start sluicing without me," I said. "You can fly on in to Anchorage and pick up Audrey and me tomorrow morning."

We drove our van to the businesses we owed money and settled up. I even stopped to see Winton Henry. It was a relief to hear that my partners had gone ahead and paid him. Then we picked up needed supplies including a new tablecloth for the kitchen and a curtain for the bedroom window to replace the one bears had clawed at over the years.

In the morning, we picked up fresh meat and met Tommy at the airport at the time we'd agreed upon, and loaded the airplane. There was lots to get on board, including cable, acetylene for welding, and oxygen. We also filled the belly and wing tanks with gas.

"Do you think we're overloading the airplane?" I asked Tommy.

He shrugged. "I don't think it'll be a problem," he said.

I parked the van and we climbed aboard the airplane. Audrey sat up in front with Tommy, and I sat behind them, surrounded by the supplies. We took off out of Anchorage. It took a long time, it seemed to me, to get airborne. We flew out across the inlet and headed north.

To get to the other side of the Alaska Range, we'd fly through Hell's Gate at about seven thousand feet. The pass has a bad reputation: lots of small planes have gone down there. Some crashes were due to weather, others to overloading.

Below us, rivers cut silvery ribbons in the lush green sweep of hills and valleys. As we flew along the Alaska Range, we saw white Dall sheep on the mountainsides— curly-horned rams and ewes. The scenery was magnificent.

Our airplane started—slowly, slowly—to gain altitude to go through Hell's Gate. I could smell the engine. I looked over Tommy's shoulder and saw the heat gauge swinging up to the red mark. The oil pressure had dropped back. The engine was starting to overheat. Beads of sweat had formed on Tommy's forehead—and on mine.

Meanwhile, Audrey was totally engrossed in watching the Dall sheep on the mountain ridges. They seemed nearly close enough to touch in this thousand-foot-wide section of the pass.

I swallowed and hoped Lady Luck was along on this ride. It seemed to me that we were clearing the pass only fifty feet above sheer rock. Hell's Gate is about seven hundred to eight hundred feet long. You come out of the pass into a valley that immediately drops off to four thousand or five thousand feet. You never know what the weather is going to be like on that side of the pass; often, the wind is high and blowing hard.

My muscles tensed, as if that would lighten our load. We slid on through the pass. No monster wind tossed and heaved our little airplane when we came out on the other side. We made it! We were going to be okay! I watched Tommy pull out a handkerchief and wipe his face.

A couple of minutes passed. "You know, Otis, I think we should have left some of that cable and other stuff behind," he said. "I'm not going to fly through Hell's Gate loaded so heavy ever again."

"Did you see the Dall sheep?" Audrey asked. "We were so close you could practically look into their eyes. What beautiful, sure-footed creatures they are."

If she knew we'd been in danger, she sure didn't let on.

CHAPTER 13

Emergency

Our Beaver airplane neared the Bear Creek mine in late afternoon. I looked down, expecting to see the boys sluicing, but there wasn't any sign of activity down below.

"That's odd," I said to Audrey. "I don't see anyone out working in the cut."

"Maybe there's been a breakdown," she said.

We landed and started unloading our gear. Dingo bounded up the trail, barking a welcome. A few minutes later, Tim came running up the trail.

"Otis and Audrey," he yelled. "Come down to the camp right away! There's been an accident."

I dropped the cable I was lugging off the plane. Audrey and I took off toward camp with Tim.

"What on earth happened?" I asked.

"Andy backed over a steep bank with the loader. It looked like it was going to tip over so he jumped out. He landed wrong. I think his ankle is broken."

Andy was stretched out on a bunk in the bunkhouse. Someone had slit his jean leg open. His ankle, badly swollen, rested on pillows. His eyes looked glassy.

105

"My ankle hurts like hell, Otis," he said. "I guess I probably broke something."

Audrey headed for the cookshack to fetch some pain pills she kept in a first aid kit.

"We tried to radio out for help," Tim said. "But we couldn't get through to anybody."

The boys had gotten the loader pulled out of the mud and brought it up to the bunkhouse.

"Put a mattress in the bucket," I said. "Then put Andy on it and get him up to the airstrip so Tommy can fly him to McGrath. I know there's a commercial flight leaving for Anchorage pretty soon, and Tommy can radio flight service and let them know there's an injured man coming in. I'll go on up ahead and help Tommy finish unloading the airplane."

We got Andy settled as comfortably as we could in the airplane. Tommy radioed the flight service and when they landed in McGrath, a stretcher and a social services nurse were waiting for Andy. The nurse gave him a shot for the pain, and they got him on the commercial flight to Anchorage. There, he was immediately transported to the hospital.

I phoned Andy in the hospital the next day. It turned out he had chipped a bone in his ankle and would be out of the mining picture for a time. Meanwhile, we continued on with our sluicing.

One evening after dinner, I heard a roar over the cookhouse—an airplane that sounded like it was about to tear off the cookshack roof. I ran outside. It was Shany West showing off a rebuilt Beaver airplane he'd managed to acquire.

"That cocky fool!" said one of the boys. It didn't speak much for West's sense of judgment to be playing daredevil games in his airplane. Buzzing our camp was silly and not a bit funny. Some of his antics in the past had caused hard feelings with the crew. Like last fall when we'd closed up the camp and needed a ride to McGrath. Shany West had radioed us that he was coming to pick us up, then he flew over and didn't stop. And his irresponsibility last spring—when he and Andy partied instead of bringing in the dragline parts—didn't engender goodwill with me or the crew. We'd had to really push to get the dragline up and working in time to mine this season since the parts came in so late.

That evening, the boys went out to do some target shooting as they often did after dinner. Well, half an hour or so later, West came in buzzing our camp again, even lower this time. I did hear some rifle shots at about the same time, but knew that the boys were target shooting.

The next day, when Tommy picked up his load of fuel in McGrath, the flight service called him in. They had a tape of a call Shany West had made to them: "I'm in trouble over Bear Creek. I think someone's shooting at me."

A few days later, I rode into McGrath with Tommy and went to the flight service and talked to West. He asked me if I knew of any shooting that had been going on that night. I told him there'd been some target practice going on but that I didn't think anyone was shooting at his airplane.

"Well, I'm sure I saw someone at the corner of your bunkhouse fire at me with a high-powered rifle," he said.

"As far as I know, the fellows were just shooting at their targets," I said. "I'll sure ask them about it when I get to camp. But I'll tell you this, Shany, flying low over our camp like you did was certainly a darn fool thing to do."

Back at the camp, I did ask my crew if any of them had fired at West's Beaver. No one stepped forward to confess. So I delivered a lecture on the bad spot we all could have been in if someone had fired at Shany West and caused him to crash. I finished my talk by telling them to handle firearms responsibly while on my mining crew.

Whether one of my boys momentarily lost his head or whether Shany West was telling a tall tale to get even with me for firing him last spring, I still don't know. But I do know that the townspeople had a lot of fun about the incident.

"Sounds to me like your boys out at Bear Creek have pretty poor aim when they're target shooting," was what I'd hear when I went in to use the pay phone in the bar. That and, "I suppose it's harder to hit a moving airplane than a cement mixer, huh, Otis?"

When Andy was ready to be discharged from the hospital in Anchorage, he flew to McGrath. We went in and got him settled in a house in town. That went pretty smoothly, thanks to Tommy. He and another fellow had rented a house in town; they offered to let Andy do his recuperating there.

"I'll be back out to work on the mine in a few more weeks, Otis," Andy said. He looked rested and seemed in good spirits.

I was glad that Andy was on the mend. So far, we'd gotten through the accidents at the mining camp okay. Every now and then, I'd see that pair of ravens flying around the camp and remember old Polly's warning about the death hex. I don't listen to lots of superstitious prattle, but out here in the Bush, it pays to be careful.

CHAPTER 14

Rumor and Revelation

Tommy flew in with fuel one morning and came out to where I was sluicing to deliver a message: "Andy says he's ready to come back out to the camp."

"Good!" I grinned. "Thanks for coming out to tell me, Tommy. I want you to go into McGrath later today and pick up parts for the big pump. You can bring Andy out when you come back."

Jeff was running the loader and I was taking charge of the water flow. I kept on working and when I looked up from the sluice box, I was surprised to see Tommy still standing there.

"Is there something else, Tommy?" I yelled above the noise of the loader.

"Yes, there is, Otis," he said, shifting from one foot to the other. "Ah, well, I've got some things I need to tell you."

"Will it wait until later?" I asked.

He nodded. "But I need to talk to you alone, Otis."

109

"Maybe we'll have time to talk at lunch," I said. I wondered what was on Tommy's mind, but sluicing took all of my attention. I liked the looks of what I was seeing in the sluice box. Even without cleaning up, I knew we were mining a good piece of ground. I couldn't help but grin while I worked. The weather had held up well this season: there'd been fewer floods. By now, we had the kinks ironed out of running the machinery and the retorting process. I was feeling good about this season.

We took a short lunch break that day so there wasn't time to talk to Tommy until he came back with the pump parts and Andy. When I came into camp that evening, Tommy motioned for me to come with him. When the boys headed in to get cleaned up for dinner, Tommy and I walked up the trail toward the airstrip by ourselves.

"I'd just about rather do anything but tell you this," Tommy said, clearing his throat a couple of times. "I feel like a spy or something, but I figure you've got to know."

"I've got to know what?" I said.

Tommy looked around, making sure we really were alone. "Did you know I've got a roommate in my house in town, Otis?"

"Yes. I met him when Andy moved in."

"Well, he spent a lot of time around the house while Andy was there. And he overheard Andy making telephone calls. Well, my roommate wouldn't have thought anything of that except he heard Andy saying stuff about you and what's been going on out at the camp. It didn't ring true to my buddy's ears, so he told me what he'd overheard. I told him no way was that true. Well, evidently there were quite a few of those phone calls. My buddy told me he figured out that Andy was talking to the White Wolf Mining people back in International Falls, Minnesota."

"Tommy, that's really hard for me to believe," I said, feeling a painful wrenching in my gut. "In fact, I don't know if I can believe it at all. Why would Andy want to lie about what's happening here?"

"Beats me, Otis," Tommy shrugged. "I just thought you should know what my buddy told me. One thing's for sure, I haven't been looking forward to bringing this news to you."

We walked a little farther, then stopped. I looked hard into Tommy's eyes, and he returned the gaze just as steadily. Instinct told me this guy was being honest with me.

"I need to think about this by myself awhile, Tommy," I said. "It comes as a terrible shock to me. You go on in and tell Audrey I'm walking up to the airstrip to bring down some parts you brought in. She can put dinner on the table if it's ready. I'll be along in a little while."

I walked up to the airstrip. It was quiet except for the whisper of aspen leaves in a gentle breeze that'd come up. I took in some deep breaths of air. It smelled clean and fresh. What should I do? I thought about the time when Andy left for a few weeks last year and about Andy and Shany West not bringing the parts in last spring. Maybe Andy harbored bad feelings about some of that. And Andy certainly knew that the former White Wolf Mining Corporation chairman and I had a parting of the ways—after all, Andy wrote letters to the corporation for me last season and we'd talked about my difficulties with the corporation officers.

Could I just leave things as they stood now? Pretend I'd never heard Tommy's words and go back to working with Andy as if nothing at all had occurred?

I asked myself those questions as I started back down the trail toward camp. By the time I got to the cookshack, I had answered those questions for myself.

The boys were still at the table nursing their last cup of coffee. "Sit down, Otis," Audrey said. "I waited to eat with you."

Pretty soon, the boys headed back to the bunkhouse. Andy was joking with them about his stay in the hospital as they left. I didn't have much of an appetite for Audrey's good spaghetti.

Of course, she knew something was up. I expected she would. "Want to talk about whatever's eating at you?" she asked. I took a swig of coffee and said, "Yes, but not right now. First, there's something I need to do."

I headed out toward the bunkhouse. Andy was standing outside.

"Andy, you and I need to have a little chat," I said. "Come on over by the toolshed."

"What's up, Otis?" Andy asked, leaning up against the shed.

"That's what I hope you'll tell me," I said. "I hear that you've been in touch with White Wolf Mining investors, talking about what's going on in camp. Is that true?"

Andy shook his head, keeping his eyes on the ground. "Why would I do that, Otis?"

"I don't know why, Andy. All I know is that I can't figure out what is going on. Now, if you've got comments to make about the happenings around here, well, you're certainly entitled to your own opinion. I just wish you'd air your grievances to me. Is there anything you want to tell me?"

"Don't have any grievances, Otis," Andy said. He still wouldn't meet my eyes. I didn't like the feel of this conversation at all.

"I may regret my decision, Andy. That I know. But the way things stand now, I feel that I've just got to let you go."

"But I just got back. I thought you needed me on the crew."

I took a deep breath. "I'll have to get along without you. I just think that we aren't going to be able to work together with trust after this. I don't know what's true and what isn't, but I can't afford to let our difficulties sour what's left of this season. It's hard enough to keep going even when everyone's 100 percent behind our effort."

Andy didn't have a lot more to say, and neither did I. I told him I did appreciate the good work he'd done and I'd pay his full wage for the time he put in.

"You gather up your gear and your tools, Andy, and

Tommy will fly you to McGrath in the morning," I said as he walked away.

I went back into the cookhouse with a sick feeling in my stomach. Audrey was about done cleaning up. She took one look at me, gave me a sugar cookie and some coffee, and said, "Now I want to know what's happened."

So I told her.

"Oh, Otis, that makes me feel awful," she said. Her eyes brimmed with tears. "I think you had to do what you did, but I wish it could have worked out differently."

"So do I, Audrey," I said. "So do I."

Audrey got the coffeepot and refilled our cups. Neither of us talked for awhile, just sat there at the cookhouse table.

I shook my head. "You know, I can't understand why any investor would get involved with Andy and try to disrupt the mine. I don't know who it is, but he surely doesn't know what he's doing. This operation could fall apart any minute. I'm doing all I can to hold it together, but then something like this pops up."

Audrey reached over and patted my hand. "Well, maybe things *will* get better with Andy out of here. Tommy's been doing your bookwork and you and the boys are getting along okay."

"Well, I am going to call International Falls tomorrow and let them know that Andy's leaving," I said. "If they want to listen to his story at a board meeting, they can go ahead and do that."

Then I recalled something.

"Audrey, do you remember last year when a guy flew in here in a small Super Cub?"

"Do you mean that fellow who'd been a miner himself?"

I nodded. "Right. He'd been in a couple of corporation-owned mining ventures. He warned me: 'When you get this thing going and everything looks good and you're getting gold out, Otis, make sure you have every receipt for every dollar you've ever spent. I've been through two of these. As soon as the thing starts paying off, somebody in that corporation is going to get the idea that he can do the job himself.'"

"It sounds like he was pretty bitter," Audrey said.

"I thought so at the time," I said. "But now I'm beginning to think there might be more than a little truth in that fellow's words."

I had a hard time sleeping that night. I listened to the wind rattle the tin siding. The old cookhouse's creaks and sighs reminded me of the first night I'd spent out here with old Jim Hunter. The ache in my gut was still with me from the afternoon. What's going to happen next? I stared into the darkness and heard Dingo whimper in his sleep out in the kitchen.

CHAPTER 15

A Big Scare

Tommy got a notice to bring the airplane to Anchorage for the annual inspection. He left for Anchorage on July 3 and would return on the fifth, bringing a load of fuel when he came.

The night of the third, after supper, Audrey suddenly doubled over. "Otis, something is very wrong with me," she gasped. "I have a terrible pain in my side."

The pain didn't go away. Audrey curled up on the bed, moaning. I knew we had to get her to a doctor. But our airplane was in Anchorage! I got on the radio: no answer. I couldn't call out at all—no contact with Anchorage or anyplace else.

"I'm hiking over to Colorado Creek to get David," Tim said and took off.

I kept our radio on; at least we could listen to the McGrath station. Shortly after Tim left, I heard a radio message for David Strant: "Get over to Yankee Creek immediately. Your father is having a heart attack."

"Oh, my God," I said. "What next?"

A few minutes later, I heard an airplane and rushed out-side. It was David's Super Cub going over at full speed, headed for Yankee Creek.

I stayed close to Audrey. She looked awful, and I was desperate! "Otis, if I lay on my right side, the pain is not quite so bad," she told me. I'd never felt more helpless in my life.

I kept trying to call out on our radio. Three hours later, Tim came back alone. "No one is at Strants'," he said. "They must all have gone to town for the Fourth of July." Of course, he didn't know about David's father.

Tim took over on the radio. Finally, at 3 A.M., he reached the Anchorage radio station. I got on right away: "This is Otis Hahn. We've got an emergency out at Bear Creek. My wife's in terrible pain. We need to get an airplane out here. Will you call Ace Airway in McGrath and ask them to send someone as soon as they can?"

"No chance of getting Ace Airway at this time of night, Mr. Hahn. But I will call at 7 A.M. and keep calling until I get an airplane on its way out to you."

Audrey was still in severe pain. Every now and then, she got up and walked. She was trying everything she could do to get even a few seconds of relief. Her face was deadly white. What would I do if she didn't pull through this? I paced the floor, trying to hide how upset I was. Life without Audrey? No, dear God, no!

At 7 A.M., thirteen hours after Audrey's pain started, there was a message on the McGrath radio: "Mr. Hahn. Ace Airway has a plane flying to Bear Creek. Get Mrs. Hahn up to your airstrip."

Tim was almost as frantic as I was. He helped me get Audrey into the bucket of the loader, cushioned with pil-lows to try to make her comfortable. Slowly, slowly, I drove the loader through the cut and up the trail to the airstrip.

Minutes after we got there, Ace Airway came in. Audrey grimaced with pain as I settled her in the airplane. I climbed in and we flew to McGrath.

A nurse met us at the airport, but there wasn't much she could do to help. We caught a commercial flight at 10 A.M., landed in Anchorage, and took a taxi to the clinic.

They took X-rays, and I held Audrey's hand while we waited for the doctor.

"I believe you have a gallstone, Mrs. Hahn," the doctor said. "You will need to have surgery."

Audrey's grip on my hand tightened. "Not here, Otis. I don't want to have the surgery here," she said.

"Would it be safe for her to fly to Minnesota for the surgery? Can it wait a few days?" I asked.

"Your wife will be uncomfortable, but she is in no immediate danger," the doctor answered.

Audrey got pain medication, and back to the airport we went. By telephone, I arranged for Dave to meet her when she landed in Minnesota. And my sister-in-law June set it up so Audrey could go directly into St. Mary's Hospital in Duluth. After that, I called Tommy.

"It seems like every time something happens, the airplane is not at the mine," he said. "I feel really bad about not being there to help Audrey."

I told him I'd be riding back to Bear Creek with him. Then we waited for Audrey's evening flight time. She was still in pain, and I felt pretty low, too.

"At least you'll be safe and in good hands," I said. "I'll try to call you on the camp radio phone. I'll have Brent come in to help out with cooking, so we'll be okay. And I'll leave the McGrath radio on to listen for messages. I want to know when you're having the surgery."

I put Audrey on the airplane and watched it take off. "Stay with us, Lady Luck," I whispered. "Let Audrey be okay."

On July 6, I got a Bush message over the McGrath radio: "Audrey is scheduled for surgery today. We'll keep you informed, Mr. Hahn."

I couldn't keep my mind on my work. That night during dinner, we got the next message: "To Otis and all the boys at Bear Creek. Audrey Hahn says she came through the surgery and is doing fine."

The boys and I kept trying to reach the hospital on the camp phone. On July 7, I was out working on machinery when Brent came tearing out of the cookhouse: "I got through! I've got St. Mary's on the line. You can talk to Audrey."

I raced inside and grabbed the mike. "How are you, Honey?" I asked.

"I'm doing fine," Audrey answered. "People here are treating me very well. The doctors have me up and walking."

"Boy, is it ever good to talk to you, Audrey. These have been very long days."

"They've been long for me, too. I miss you, and I've been wondering about David's dad. Have you talked to David?"

"Yes. David said they got his dad to Anchorage, and he's going to pull through."

"That's good news. Otis, I'll go home and rest up and be back in camp in a couple of weeks. You just take good care of yourself and keep the bear out of the bedroom."

I chuckled. Audrey sounded great!

CHAPTER 16

Winding Up
the Second Season

The third week of July, Audrey flew back to Bear Creek looking healthy and rested. It was really good to have her back. I hadn't heard from any of the White Wolf Mining officers in many weeks. After Andy left, I tried to call the chairman on our radio-phone but never did get through. I worried and stewed about the situation, losing lots of sleep at night.

"Otis, you look all tuckered out," Tim told me one afternoon when we were sluicing together. "Maybe you're working too many hours."

"Tim, physical work has never bothered me," I told him. "It's the corporation end of this thing that's keeping me awake nights."

Some nights I'd pace back and forth in the cookhouse kitchen, trying to figure out some way to get the officers' cooperation. Food had quit tasting so good to me, too.

"For heaven's sake, Otis, it isn't going to help matters for you to get all worked up over that mining corporation board," Audrey called out to me from the bedroom at one in the morning. I'd been pacing in the kitchen from the sink to the door, back and forth, back and forth.

"I know you're right," I said. "But my mind keeps getting caught up in it, wondering what really is going on."

Audrey got out of bed, pulled on a sweater, and came into the cookhouse kitchen. "I'll make some hot chocolate for us."

In a small pan, she heated water on the stove, added powdered milk, spooned some hot chocolate powder into two cups, and added the steaming liquid. We sat down at the table.

"Now, tell me what exactly is rolling around in your head," she said. "I think it'll help you to talk this thing out."

So I did. I told her it seemed to me that the investors were still sitting back, letting me deal with everything without any support. They were even less communicative than last year. And then there was the episode with Andy.

"You know, Audrey, I've tried to do my part, sending them reports on our progress when I could. I just don't understand why they don't keep in touch and don't do what they say they're going to do. That puzzles me. Last spring, one investor said that some of the corporation board resent me because I run the mine like I own it. Well, as far as I can see, that's the only way to make this operation go. Maybe this is just a lark to them, while it's very serious business to those of us who are up here."

I blew on the hot chocolate to cool it down and talked between sips, the cup warming in my hands. The smell of the warm chocolate and milk was comforting.

"I guess my partners know I'll work really hard because I've got my money in this mine along with theirs. I certainly don't want to lose my investment. And we've done really well. This season, I've already cashed in close to 200 ounces of gold; there's another 125 ounces on hand, and we've still got a couple of cleanups ahead of us. It looks like all the expenses are going to be picked up this second year, plus the corporation will be getting some money back."

Audrey nodded, sipping her hot chocolate and listening.

"Well, Audrey, the question is, where do we go from here? This corporation is not working out the way it's supposed to. Now we've got some bitter feelings in the mix, too. I don't mind working hard, you know that better than anyone. But I do mind walking around with this ache in my insides and feeling abandoned by the mining corporation board. That's eating away at me. This is no way to exist."

Our cups were empty. Audrey put them in the sink. Dingo was sound asleep under the kitchen table.

"You'll know what's the right course of action for you to take, Otis," Audrey said, patting my shoulder. "I know it will come to you. But for now, let's just go to bed."

I slept pretty well. The hot chocolate and the talking must have helped.

The next day was clear and bright. Audrey was frying bacon when I came out of the bedroom. I saw that she'd curled her hair and had put lipstick on. I hadn't been noticing things like that for a long time. Sweet Audrey, I thought to myself, still looking darn good after all these years.

"You look nice this morning, Audrey," I said.

She wasn't one to hang on a compliment. "Oh, well, every now and then I have to do something to keep my spirits up out here, too," she said, dropping spoonfuls of batter onto the pancake griddle.

That made me stop and think. This mining venture had been hard for her to go through. It was mid-August and she had worked as hard as the rest of us.

That night after supper, Audrey said, "Otis, I've got a suggestion. Why don't you and I and the boys take a day off and go fishing? Early this season, you talked about going up to Graham Creek for grayling. You haven't done that yet. You've been working from early morning until night since April. I think all of us could use a day off."

I thought about that. My crew had been hard workers all season long. I liked Audrey's suggestion.

"You know, I think that's just what we'll do."

I went over to the bunkhouse and made an announcement. "Fellows, we're going to do something different tomorrow."

They sat on their bunks and waited to hear what I had in mind.

"Tomorrow's a day off with pay. You can do what you want to do. Myself, I'm going fishing for those grayling. If you want to come along, you're sure welcome to."

"That's great," they said, practically in unison. Frank and Tim were especially enthusiastic. "This is our chance to go up on Cripple Mountain. All summer we've been talking about going up and walking on the mountain ridge," said Tim. The mountain was east of us about two miles.

Later that evening, the boys fired up the sauna. I'd gone into the cookhouse and was getting my fishing gear ready. I heard someone yell "Fire!" I looked out the window and saw smoke pouring out of the sauna, so I grabbed a five-gallon pail that Audrey had filled with water earlier that day. I ran out to the sauna and threw the water into the sauna door. This time, Tim was the one who got drenched.

"Hey, Otis," he yelled, "did you think I was on fire?"

I laughed. We doused the sauna interior with more water and got the fire out, although it left a good-sized hole in the floor. Every so often, you could count on that sauna to create a little excitement around camp.

The next day, Audrey and I took off on foot for Graham Creek. It felt good just to stretch out and walk and be doing something besides mining for one day. The woods we walked through smelled of spruce. Sunshine danced on the creek and warmed the air. We sat on the bank without talking for a long while—just watched the water run by and enjoyed being together on our day off. It also gave me a chance to do some thinking about the mine. That morning, all of sudden, it came to me. I knew what I was probably going to do about the White Wolf Mining Corporation board. There were still things I needed to sort out, but at least I had the beginnings of a plan.

"Otis, I think I've got a big one this time," Audrey said after we'd been at one spot an hour or so. On the end of her line was a grayling that measured close to twenty-four inches.

The fish we caught tasted mighty good when Audrey and I fried them up for supper that night. Talk around the dinner table was relaxed and easy. Audrey had pulled in the biggest fish, and I took some kidding about that. Then the fellows started to talk about what they'd do when they got to town. Actually, it was more which girls they were interested in seeing.

It was my turn to kid them back. "I get a kick out of you boys," I said. "When you're out here, there's all this talk about what'll happen when you get to town. Then, when you find yourself with some cute girl in town, all you talk about is what's going on out at the mine."

Audrey was absolutely right: that day off did all of us lots of good. The next morning, we went back to sluicing. Tommy brought in the mail along with the fuel. There was a letter from Dave and one from our hometown bank in Minnesota.

It's a good thing I'd had that day of fishing to come to better terms with where I stood regarding White Wolf Mining, because the news in those letters wasn't good. Audrey opened them up and read them to me. The bank letter notified us that we'd used up our line of credit on the farm; they would give us no more money to keep the farm operation going. Dave's letter told us that hog prices were still down and that things had not improved over the summer. The farm situation had been at the back of my mind all along. I knew that I'd have to make a decision when I came back in the fall. Dave and I couldn't afford to go into debt any further.

The season was slowly coming to a close. The nip in the morning air and the yellow-tinged aspen leaves signaled that it was time to start thinking about leaving. The old cow moose was still around camp. Her calves had made it through the summer and were almost as big as their mother now. Pretty soon the sluice box would be freezing at night.

I had more than two hundred ounces of gold in camp now and still had some in the sluice box. When the box started freezing and we couldn't get back to sluicing until 10 A.M., I decided to call it a season. We picked up another eighty ounces in the final cleanup and got the equipment put away for the winter.

At the breakfast table one morning in late August, the boys and I talked about the ivory we'd collected. "Tommy, maybe we should let you take the ivory to Anchorage and store it at your place until we find a market, if that's all right with you and the rest of the boys," I said. "We don't know what's coming up for next year. I'd feel a lot safer with the ivory at Tommy's place. Tim can come up with a market for it, and we'll divide the money into equal shares when we sell it."

"Sure, Otis," Tommy agreed. The other crew members thought that sounded like a good plan.

Audrey had been packing for two weeks. I had Tommy fly me over to Colorado Creek to say good-bye to David Strant. "I want to thank you for the help you've given us all along, David," I said.

"It's been a pleasure to have you as a neighbor," David said, pumping my hand. "Hope you have a good winter in Minnesota."

My plan was to have Tommy fly us to McGrath. With all of our gear plus my dog Dingo, it would take two trips. After we stored the airplane in McGrath for the winter, we'd catch a commercial flight to Anchorage, and the rest of the crew would fly back to the Lower 48. Audrey and I would drive the van back to Minnesota.

Tommy took the boys out first. Audrey, Dingo, and I flew out in the second flight. As the red-and-white Beaver climbed up out of the valley, I took a good long look at the camp down below—the battered old buildings, the cut we'd just finished working, our little airstrip. I felt a real fondness for the place. Leaving this year was different from last year. Audrey was flying out with me, for one thing. But it still wasn't easy to say farewell. I kept the mine in sight as long as I could. More than two years' worth of my heart and soul were down below, in that gold mine on Bear Creek.

CHAPTER 17

Going Home

When we got to McGrath, old Jim Hunter was at the airport. I had his share of the gold in a little poke. He was all smiles when I handed it to him. He hefted it up and down. "I'd guess it's at least ten thousand dollars' worth, Otis."

The old fellow knew his gold: that's exactly what was in the poke! A crowd had gathered to say good-bye. We stood around awhile and talked to people. When we walked over to the airport to get on the commercial flight to Anchorage, Jim followed us. I shook his hand.

"Well, I'll see you in the spring," I said.

"Don't be too sure of that, Otis," Jim said. "I'm running out of daylight, my friend."

Jim reached down and patted Dingo on the head and watched us board the plane.

Dogs are supposed to be in a crate during flight, but there weren't many passengers, and the pilot knew us by now. He'd seen us come into the airport and yelled to me, "Otis, don't bother about a crate. Dingo can sit with you up in the front of the plane." So Dingo sat between Audrey and me, wagging his tail.

We checked into a motel in Anchorage. Audrey went out shopping for things to bring back for the grandchildren, and I called the McGrath radio station to thank them for helping us this season. I really appreciated that Bush radio station.

Before the boys left Anchorage, they came to our room to say good-bye.

"It's been a real adventure, Otis," Frank told me. "I'll probably never have the opportunity to do something like this again."

The next morning, in a drizzly rain, we loaded up the van. With a thermos full of hot black coffee, Audrey, Dingo, and I left Anchorage at 4:30 A.M. Dingo had spent the night in the van so he was glad to see us. He jumped up in the front seat beside me.

"I'm sitting by Otis, not you," Audrey laughed and put him in the back seat. He put his front paws on the seat back, licked my ear, and put his head on my shoulder. I chuckled and told him, "Well, I know you're excited, fella, but it'll be a mighty long trip back to Minnesota with you behaving this way."

Audrey slept for the next few hours. "Where are we, Otis?" she asked when she opened her eyes.

"Not far from Tok Junction," I said. "We'll stop for breakfast there."

"I couldn't figure out where I was when I woke up. It's good to know that I don't have to cook breakfast for a crew."

Tok Junction is where you get on the Alaska Highway; if you turn north, it's about two hundred miles to Fairbanks. We headed south through Canada's Yukon to British Columbia where the Alaska Highway ends at Dawson Creek, some thirteen hundred miles from Tok.

The sun came out from behind the mountains. It was a dazzling sight, the forested hills turned bright fall gold.

"The Alaska Highway is really good now," Audrey said. "I remember it back in the 1950s, when it was rocks, holes, and bumps for fifteen hundred miles."

While we drove, I talked about some of the happenings in camp Audrey'd missed because of her gallstone surgery— like the night that Jim Hunter's son, Jack, landed on our airstrip. The boys and I heard the plane coming in and thought something didn't sound quite right with it. Well, Tommy and the rest of the fellows ran up to the airstrip. I'd been in bed, so it took me awhile to get dressed. On my way up to the airstrip, I heard the plane take off. It passed over me about three hundred feet in the air; finally, it gained altitude. The boys came down the trail. They said Jack Hunter, who was working at the Strants', had been drinking and took off in one of David's airplanes. When he landed on our strip, the prop cut trenches all the way along our runway. He'd ended up down between those two old tractor frames.

The boys pulled him back onto the airstrip and told Jack to get out of the airplane, but he was in a fighting mood and wouldn't budge. The prop was all bent back, but he took off anyway.

Well, we watched him flying back toward Colorado Creek. A few days later, David told me that Jack landed the plane there but had caused thirty-five hundred dollars' damage to it. So lots of his summer wages were going to go toward paying for the repair.

Audrey laughed. "Another crazy thing that happened in that mining camp."

We took turns driving and passed through Canadian customs at Beaver Creek, which was built up a lot from when Audrey'd last seen it. Snowcapped peaks jutted up around Kluane Lake. It's a breathtaking sight, and the lake is different shades of blue at different times of the day. We spotted Dall sheep grazing on the mountainsides. Kluane National Park holds Canada's highest mountains and the largest population of Dall sheep in the world. This is one of my favorite spots in the Yukon.

We stopped for the night in Whitehorse and drove into British Columbia the next day. Beyond Dawson Creek, we ran into farmland. Combining was going on. We drove by a hog-raising operation and Audrey chuckled.

"Otis, I remember when Dave had that big sow that was having trouble giving birth and someone told him if you give the sow a beer, it would speed things along."

"I remember that," I said. "Dave went to town and got a six-pack of beer and went out in the hog house. Well, I went out at 1 A.M., and there was Dave, sound asleep on the hay bales with an empty six-pack beside him. The sow was laying there with eleven little pigs nursing. I woke Dave up and said, 'That beer must have worked pretty good.' He told me, 'I guess so, and I sure got a good rest, too.'"

We drove through Alberta and Saskatchewan. Grain elevators topped the prairie horizon, and dust rose from the combines in the fields. Everywhere, big piles of wheat were stored outside—a bad sign for anyone expecting wheat prices to go up.

At 10:30 p.m., we were in Kenora, Ontario. If we headed straight south, we were about a five-hour drive from home. But I wanted to go through customs at International Falls and drop off all my receipts and papers for the year at White Wolf Mining. Audrey called our daughter, Linda, and told her we'd be home around one or two the next afternoon.

We got to International Falls around 10 A.M. I took the papers to the White Wolf Mining accountant. He said he was glad to see me but didn't seem overly enthusiastic. I told him we'd gotten almost five hundred ounces of gold this season.

"I'll give you a full report at the next meeting. You can let the investors know I'm back, and then call me with the meeting date."

When we got to the farm in Mizpah, the yard was full of cars. Neighbors along with our family were there to greet us. We all hugged one another. The grandkids made a big fuss over us and Dingo. It was a real homecoming!

"Did you really shoot a bear in your underwear, Grandpa?" asked little Shane as soon as he could get a word in.

"I sure did," I said.

"Was he showing his big old teeth, Grandpa?"

I told him how the bear broke through the window.

"Was Dingo scared?"

"You bet he was!" I said. "And so was your grandpa."

CHAPTER 18

The Farm
and Hard Decisions

The grandkids were excited about showing us a fort they'd built in the woods behind the house. So Audrey and I walked out there with them.

"Oh, Otis, the pines smell so good," Audrey said, taking a deep breath. "It is nice to be home."

The kids had small poles leaning up against some trees: that was the fort. They got inside and pretended we were attacking them. Their laughter and make-believe were welcome after a summer in the Alaska Bush.

Everybody helped us unload the van. Later, the grandkids, Audrey, and I drove over to the farrowing barns. An old Dodge pickup came down the road. The driver was my long-time friend Allen Murray. We grew up together, have been neighbors for as far back as I can remember, and have hunted and tramped the North Woods together all our lives.

We slowed down and stopped alongside each other.

"Well, if it isn't the old gold miner back from Alaska," Allen grinned. "I'll be over to hear your stories, Otis."

On the way to the farrowing barns, we stopped by the cattle pasture. I got out of the van and called out to the cattle. They came over to the fence. They still knew my voice. I saw old Ruthie with her new calf.

Audrey started telling the grandkids about the time we saved Ruthie's calf in a surprise snowstorm on May 1. The cattle had gotten out, and Ruthie gave birth to a calf in a snowbank. We went out and found the calf, carried it back to the barn, dried it off, and it was just fine.

We'd forgotten to close the van door. Suddenly, Dingo leaped out of the van, ran into the pasture barking, and started chasing the cattle.

They bellowed at him. Finally, I caught him and got him back in the van. We'd had trouble with Dingo chasing cattle last winter, too. He didn't have a farm dog upbringing and figured those cattle were moose.

A flock of sharp-tailed grouse flew up from the ditch as we got close to the farrowing barns, and grandson Mike said, "My dad says we can hunt them this fall."

Believe it or not, the farrowing barn smelled good to my nose. We took pride in our sows and kept the barns clean. Neighbors told us our barns were cleaner than some folks' houses. It looked like Dave and his wife, Ann, had been doing a good job tending the sows. We all pitched in and did the evening chores and then drove back to the house.

Dave got home from work later that afternoon. He'd lost a lot of weight, and his face had the look of an old man. Right away, he hugged Audrey and me.

"Dave, you look tired," I said. He nodded and said, "I am, Dad."

He asked how things went at the mine.

I told him very little had changed with the corporation. "In fact, I'd say there was even less cooperation and support from the investors this year."

"What was the deal with Andy?" Dave asked. "He came back and hung around here for awhile. I asked him, 'What happened? Did you just leave Dad up there?' He said, 'I just couldn't put up with it anymore. I got tired of it, so I left.'"

I told Dave the story, and he nodded. "I knew there had to be more to it than what Andy said."

My son-in-law Curt had been listening to us talk. "Well, as long as you're on the subject, I might as well tell you that I heard through the grapevine that Andy had a meeting with the White Wolf Mining people."

"If he did, it wouldn't surprise me," I said. "Andy was upset about lots of things, including my hiring Tommy instead of him to do the bookwork and communicate with the board members this year. I'm sure Andy had lots of opinions about what I was doing wrong. And there were hard feelings between me and one of my partners after I wrote that letter of complaint to them about the first season. Andy may have been encouraged to report on me."

We talked until midnight and finally went to bed.

"It sure feels good to be back in our own bedroom," Audrey said. "But I still feel like I'm riding in that van."

We lay there awake for awhile. "I can't sleep," Audrey said. "It's the farm that's bothering me. What's going to happen?"

I sighed. "Probably, it'd be best to have an auction sale. I hate to say those words, but that's what we'll likely have to do."

"I suppose so. I didn't want to say it either, Otis, but I'd been thinking that, too."

The next morning, I went over to Dave's—he and Ann lived in a house near the farrowing barns. We had coffee together and I told Ann to take the morning off: I'd take over for her in the barns.

Dave and I went out to the farrowing barn and cleaned the crates. Then Dave said, "Turn on the barn cleaner, Dad. It's ready to go."

We sat down on a bale of hay. Dave took off his cap, brushed his hair back off his forehead, and smiled. "Do you remember the time when you nearly electrocuted yourself with the barn cleaner?" he asked.

"It was a close call for me," I said. "And I remember when you went to town for the beer for the sow and fell asleep out here.

"We have had good and bad times out here," I said. I paused. "And I think it's time to face up to what we need to do next, son. We are in bad shape financially. I sure don't want to tell you this, but I think that the only way out is to have an auction sale."

Dave's fingers tightened on the cap in his hand. He looked down at the floor.

"I'll go to town, Dave, and get the banker's view on the situation. I'll see what advice he has."

"Dad, Grandpa Hahn didn't have it easy out here, either."

I looked at Dave's tired, drawn face. I answered, "No, but at the end of the month, he didn't have a light bill or phone bill or car payments to meet. Back then, a gallon of kerosene for lanterns cost ten cents. So they got by. They had the bare necessities of life. Today, you've got three tractors that cost thirty thousand to forty thousand dollars apiece. They had horses and put up hay for them. Now we've got bills to pay on equipment, and they didn't. That's what puts us in a bind."

Dave just sat there, looking at the floor.

"The U.S. farm situation is bad," I said. "There are foreclosures all over the country. The ones who'll survive don't have big debts, but that's not the case for 99 percent of us."

We left the farrowing barn. The sun shone on the stubble in the fields. This land was where my dad had raised me and where I had raised my four kids. It had been a good place to live.

"Listen, Dad, the geese are coming in. There's some lower ground with quite a bit of grain left for them, but I didn't leave any swatches of grain like you always did."

The Canadian honkers circled low over the fields and

set down. We stood and watched. Then Dave said, "Mike and I went hunting last year, and we shot a goose, although I know it's against your policy."

My son Randy drove up in a pickup. He hadn't been able to come yesterday. He told me I looked healthy and told Dave a flock of seventy-five or a hundred sharp-tailed grouse flew up from the field when he drove by.

Dave smiled, "We've got over two hundred on the place. They're getting up by the grain bins. I guess we'll have to start taking a few of them. We're attracting too many."

I looked out across the fields over at the neighbor's farm. I loved standing by the farrowing barns and listening to my boys talk. I felt a wave of sadness: tomorrow I'd be in talking to the banker.

Ann came out of the house and called to me, "Otis, Audrey called and wants you to come home right away. Dingo's tangled with a porcupine."

Poor Dingo. Quills bristled on his nose. When I held him down and opened his mouth, I saw quills way back on his tongue and down his throat. We took him to the vet, and he had to put him under to get the quills out. We carried him home unconscious and put him on a blanket in the basement.

That night, we dined on grouse—the best eating there is. We sat over coffee, and my grandson Mike wanted to hear bear stories.

"I've got one for you, too," said Dave. "Last summer, I got a call from a friend with a Super Cub. He told me he flew over our farm and counted sixteen bears in the oat field. So we lost some of our crop to those bears where they tramped down oats in the field."

That night, I heard a thump, thump in the basement. Dingo had come out of the anesthetic and tried to come up the stairs but fell back down. We brought him into our bedroom, and he tried to get on the bed but couldn't. He had a couple of rough days out of his porcupine adventure.

On Monday morning, I got ready to go to the bank. Audrey walked me out of the house and put her hand on my shoulder. "Good luck, Otis," she said, her eyes bright with tears.

I discovered we had a female banker. The man I'd dealt with last year had died. Of course, I knew the woman. In a small place like this, you know almost everybody. "I drove by your farm and saw your rig in the yard last weekend, so I figured you'd be in this morning, Otis," she said as we shook hands.

"Well, I've been banking here thirty years, and I need to talk to you about our farm."

She nodded. "The interest on your loan here is past due. We had a board meeting a month ago, and your case was brought up. I don't want you to feel bad, Otis, but we are swamped with foreclosures right now. We don't know which way to turn with some of them. In your case, I told the board we didn't have anything to worry about. You've always been straightforward with us in all our dealings."

"I appreciate that," I said, "but I'm in a dilemma."

"So are lots of people, including some of your neighbors. Do you have a plan?"

I told her I was thinking about an auction sale.

She shook her head. "I've got to warn you. There've been lots of auction sales lately, and machinery is not selling very well."

"If I wait a year, do you think it will be better?"

"I don't know, but it doesn't look promising. There are foreclosures all over the United States. Maybe you're smart to get out now."

I told her David had the land now and was behind one FHA payment a year ago and another one now. Pretty big payments, too.

"What I'd like to do is release the cows and hogs off the mortgage to allow us to sell those and make the back payments plus this year's payment to the FHA. That would give

Dave a year or two to sell the land. I hate to let the land go, but I'm almost sixty years old. I really don't have much choice. All the money the machinery sale makes will go toward paying off the notes here. We have enough machinery to cover that, I believe."

She looked over my records of the machinery that I'd brought along and decided I'd be safe in doing that. And it would put Dave in a better position for selling the hog-farrowing operation.

"When will you have the sale?" she asked.

I told her I'd let her know the date. "I want to do it in early spring, because I may be going back up to Alaska."

"How's that outfit getting along, Otis?"

"Well, there are internal problems in the corporation," I answered. "But the mining itself has gone well. We got around five hundred ounces of gold this year and have ground prepared for next season."

We shook hands again. I felt a little easier about our situation when I left. At least we'd be able to hold on to the land for a year or so, and hopefully, Dave'd be able to sell it.

Well, I knew that Audrey and I'd be the big losers in this. The FHA held Dave's first mortgage on the farm, and I held the second one.

Audrey was waiting for me at home. I told her about the meeting and watched her eyes fill with tears. Suddenly, I couldn't trust my voice. I quit talking and walked into the kitchen. I opened the cupboard and got out a glass, ran some water into it, took a deep breath, put the glass to my lips, and swallowed.

I felt Audrey's hand on my shoulder. "This is hard for both of us, but I guess that's the route we'll have to take," she said. "We've both thought about it a long time, Otis."

Late in the afternoon, I went over to help Ann with chores. Dave came home looking exhausted. "This is the longest day of my life," he said. "I kept wondering what happened at the bank."

I told him how the meeting went. "The good thing is they've released the cattle and hogs so we can make the FHA loan payments. That gives you time to sell the land."

"Well, I can breathe a little easier, Dad, but it's sure not what I'd like to see happen."

"Dave, there are foreclosures all around us," I said. "You and Ann are still young. Now you can enjoy your life without living under the strain of all of this. And Audrey and I will still be here, in the farmhouse on the ten acres we separated out from the land before we turned it over to you. Not everyone is that fortunate. I know one family where the house and yard were included in the land their son got from them. Now they're losing their home. At least we have that ten acres and a house for Audrey and me."

I tried to keep sentiment out of the discussion. Dave was taking the news pretty hard, I could tell. And I didn't know of a way to make it easier on him.

"Well, we'll have plenty to do to get things ready for the auction," I said. The words sounded hollow. When the chores were done, I drove home feeling sad and empty and close to tears. This was the beginning of the end of our family farm.

CHAPTER 19

The Board Meeting

I drove over to see Allen Murray the next day. He was sitting on the porch. Good old Allen takes life day by day, and doesn't let things upset him.

I noticed his dog, Daisy, wasn't around so I asked about her.

"Well, Otis, I was out at Rapid River camping. Every night, wolves were howling around camp. I let Daisy out one night, and she didn't come back. I went out looking for her, but I couldn't find a trace of her. I figure the timber wolves got her."

Pretty soon we were swapping stories about our camping adventures and laughing. It felt good to forget about my troubles and just sit there talking about old times with Allen.

When I got home, Audrey said the trucking company called. They'd be out in the morning to haul away the cattle and hogs. I called Dave and told him. The next day dragged by. Audrey, Dave, Ann, and I got the cattle into the corral, but none of us said very much. The cattle bellowed and carried on, including old Ruthie.

Leaving a dust trail on the road, four big semis pulled up. I leaned on the fence and watched the livestock get loaded. It went fast. I had an awful lump in my throat watching the semis pull away.

The place was suddenly quiet. The corral and barns stood empty. Ann and Dave walked back to their house. Audrey didn't say a word, just stared out the pickup window when we drove home. We went into the house, and she headed straight for the bedroom. I knew she was crying. I went out in the yard and cried, too.

A few days later, a letter came from White Wolf Mining announcing a board meeting on October 25 to update investors on the past season. Meanwhile, I started repairing equipment in preparation for the sale. We scheduled a company to hold the auction on April 4. That should work out with the mining season since I wouldn't need to get up to Alaska so early next season. All of our equipment was there and ready to go.

I asked my daughter Linda's husband, Jeff, to ride up to International Falls with me on October 25 and take notes for me at the board meeting. He agreed to do that.

Not too many investors showed up that evening, a half-dozen or so. We shook hands all around. They seemed glad to see me.

Minutes of the last meeting were read, and then came the financial report. Beads of sweat broke out on my forehead: the financial report did not coincide with my reported expenses for the season. The fuel expense I'd submitted was twenty-two thousand dollars. The fuel expense in the report had been jacked up to more than double that figure. The report's airplane fare and lodging expense was for eighteen thousand dollars. The amount I'd reported was *much* less.

I started asking questions. I was told the airplane and lodging expense figure included a trip for some of the investors to go to Arizona to study thawing permafrost electrically.

"Otis, how big a light plant have we got up at Bear Creek?" asked one investor.

"Big enough to run a washing machine and three light bulbs," I said. "I don't know what you people are talking about. I haven't heard any mention of this before."

It would get rid of the permafrost, the investor said. I just shook my head. It was ridiculous; they had no idea what they were dealing with.

The meeting proceeded. Then, I brought up a suggestion, part of the plan I'd hit upon when I was fishing for grayling at Graham Creek. "I'd like to have an audit of our books and get everything brought up to date," I said.

"That's not necessary, Otis," said the chairman. "We've got an accountant in our corporation who takes care of that. There's no need to spend money on an audit to bring our books up."

"It wouldn't need to cost anything. I'll bet the IRS would be happy to come in and do the audit for no charge," I said.

Getting an outside audit of the books was obviously something they did not want to consider. Then, I updated them on the operation, told them the new sluice box worked very well and that I had ground prepared for next season.

"Our biggest expenses are behind us now," I said.

"How much will it cost to open up camp next spring?" asked the treasurer.

"About thirty-five thousand dollars for groceries, fuel, and repairs on the big tractor," I answered.

The financial report also included a twelve-hundred-dollar reimbursement to Andy for tools and equipment he reportedly left at the mine. I had a hard time staying calm enough to talk.

"How did that come about?" I asked. "All he left at the camp was a kerosene burner and not much else. That's not worth that kind of money."

The frightening thing was all the vague circle talk. I

couldn't get a direct answer to that question or most of the questions and suggestions I brought up.

The chairman was in a hurry to end the meeting. When it was over, I sat there a few minutes, stunned. One investor pulled me aside as I got ready to leave.

I looked at him and said, "I wish you'd tell me what the hell is going on here."

"I don't know either," he said.

"Well, I certainly don't agree with the financial report that I heard tonight. Did you go to the meeting with Andy?" I asked.

"Yes, but I'm not at liberty to give you any details," he said. "Otis, is it true you're illiterate?"

"Yes, but I didn't think that was any big secret here."

"Well, it certainly wasn't after the meeting with Andy. But I want you to know, I think you've done a good job for us in the mine. It's too bad things are going the way they are. If this whole thing goes sour, what are the chances of getting our investment back?"

"Very, very slim," I said. "I'd guess the very most you could get would be about ten cents to the dollar if that."

On the ride back to Mizpah, Jeff said, "I've sat in lots of board meetings, but that was the rockiest one I've attended."

"If I'd have known things were going to go like this," I said, "I wouldn't have gotten involved in the first place."

When we got home, Audrey woke up when I went into the bedroom. "How did the meeting go?" she asked.

I gave her the details and admitted I was nervous and worried about the corporation. "To tell you the truth, it scares me," I said.

"It scares me, too," she said.

That winter, I kept busy out in my shop, working on machinery. One afternoon, I heard the workshop door open, and my grandsons Shane, Kent, and Mike came in. They liked to fool around in there while I worked. I told Kent to throw a log in the barrel stove.

Shane and Mike perched on the plow. "Tell us a story, Grandpa," Mike said.

"Okay, Mike, I will," I said. I pulled myself out from under the plow, wiped the grease off my hands, and sat down by the stove. The boys got stools and sat around me.

"This story happened years ago, when my dad farmed here. He had a big barn. There were chickens, horses, and cows all in that barn. Late one fall, my brother Ray and I were trapping mink up on Lost Tamarack River. It was cold so we stopped to build a fire and cook ourselves some coffee. All of a sudden, we heard a whimpering, crying noise. It sounded sort of like a baby.

"We went to investigate. Ray walked over to an old, hollowed-out cedar log. 'The noise is coming from here,' he said. We looked in the log, and there was a little bear cub.

"'What do you think we should do?' Ray asked. I said, 'Maybe we should take him home with us.'

"Well, Ray took off his belt and reached in and put it around the bear's neck. We drank our coffee, put the fire out, and took that bear home with us. The little fellow didn't have much fight in him. We got home after dark.

"I went in the house, and Dad said, 'You boys are pretty late. You'd better get out and do your chores.' I figured this wasn't the time to tell him about the cub.

"We took the bear to the barn with us. The cattle were a little skittish but we put the cub in an empty stall at the end of the barn. We stuffed some hay in an orange crate and covered the cub up.

"'Maybe we should get him something to eat,' Ray said. 'Mom and Dad'll be in the living room, and I can probably go into the kitchen and get some bread without them hearing me.'

"So he did. Then we milked some milk from a cow into a pan and soaked the bread in it. The little bear gobbled it up. Then we covered him back up with hay and went in the house and went to bed.

"The next morning, we heard Dad get up and go out to the barn to do the chores. He came back right away. We heard him tell Mom, 'I've got a mess in the barn. All the stanchions are torn loose. The horses are loose, and the harnesses are all in the muck in the gutter. I can't figure out what's happened.'

"'Oh, oh,' I told Ray. 'It looks like we're in trouble.'"

By this point in my story, the little boys' eyes were wide. It made me grin to watch them.

"Well, we got out of bed and went to the barn with Dad. It was a mess! Ray looked up in the rafters and said, 'Look, Dad, there's a bear up there.'

"'How in the world did a bear cub get in my barn?' Dad said. Ray and I looked at each other and shrugged. Then Dad reached out and grabbed each of us by our shirt collars and said, 'You boys better come clean with me. I know that bear didn't get in here by himself.'

"We had to tell him what happened. The good thing was, he liked wild animals. The bad part was that Ray and I had to rebuild the stanchions and clean all the harnesses."

Shane was leaning forward on his stool so far that he toppled over. He laughed. "But the bear, Grandpa, what happened to the bear?" asked Mike.

"We got him down from the rafters, and my dad told us to make a den for him in a chicken coop."

"But where was his mother?" asked Shane.

"She probably got shot by a hunter. Anyway, Dad told us not to feed him, that bears hibernate in winter and it's not natural for them to eat. The little guy never did go to sleep, though, and he died a few days later. I think he was too weak to have survived, no matter what we did."

"Tell us another bear story, Grandpa," said Shane.

"I think we'd better head into the house for dinner," I said. "I'll bet Grandma's waiting for us."

As we left the workshop, the boys started singing, "Grandpa shot a bear in his underwear." I chuckled.

When we got to the house, Audrey said that I'd had a call from White Wolf Mining. "They've called an emergency meeting for March 5 at 7 P.M."

"That's tomorrow night," I said. "I wonder what's happened now?"

I drove up to International Falls the next evening. There were four or five investors present and a man from Arizona. The chairman called the meeting to order.

"Otis, we think you've lost 50 percent of the gold with the new sluice box you built," I was told.

I replied that there's not a sluice box made that doesn't lose 8 to 10 percent of the gold. "But I guarantee you that I didn't lose any 50 percent."

Then the man from Arizona pulled out some charts and went into detail about just how I was losing gold.

The upshot was they asked me to go up to Alaska with the Arizona fellow and let him get some samples from the tailing piles to see if we were losing that much gold.

"The tailing piles are frozen now. I don't know if you can even get in and out of the mine with a ski plane yet," I said.

They said I could chop some gravel out so the fellow could do some checking. I shrugged. They were determined to do this.

"Well, I've got an auction sale coming up on April 4, but I'll give you one week if that's what you really want. But you fellows will have to pay all the airfare and expenses plus a week's wages for me. I'll need a round-trip ticket to Anchorage sent to me. You've also got to pay for a round-trip ticket from Anchorage to McGrath and back, plus a ticket for Ace Airway to fly us to the mine—if we can get in at all."

It was a fool's mission, but the chairman and investors were all smiles. They looked at the Arizona fellow's charts and gathered around him. They thought that, at last, they had someone who'd really know what he was doing up there.

The board members told me the Arizona fellow would bring the money for the lodging, meals, and other expenses.

So, on March 7, I flew to Anchorage. I got in at 2 P.M. and the Arizona guy was waiting for me. We went to a motel and when we stepped up to the counter, he turned to me and asked, "Are you paying for this?"

"Hell, no," I said. "You were supposed to get money from the mining corporation. Didn't they give you the money?"

He said, "No. All they gave me was the round-trip ticket to Anchorage."

"I don't understand," I said. "You were standing right there when they said you'd have the money."

He kind of smiled and shrugged. "How much money will it take?" he asked.

"It'll be at least four hundred dollars apiece to get to Bear Creek, out to the mine, and back."

"Do you have money?" he asked.

"Mister, I never leave on a trip like this without money. Yes, I have enough to pay my costs, but that's not the way it was set up with the board. Go ahead and get the room, and I'll pay for it."

I wondered just how big an operator my board had gotten themselves hooked up with here, this man who didn't think to bring money on his first trip to Alaska. When we got to the room, I called the White Wolf Mining treasurer.

"You promised this gentleman would have the money for expenses. Well, we're sitting in Anchorage and still need to get to Bear Creek."

He said there must have been a mix-up.

"There certainly must have been. For my part, I can get on the airplane and come right back to Minnesota. What do you want me to do?"

He offered to wire us money. I said, "No," knowing it'd take him two or three days to get around to doing it, if not longer!

"I left a thousand dollars in our Anchorage bank account last fall," I told him. "I'll draw that out and use it to cover the rest of the trip."

"It's a good thing you left the thousand dollars there," the treasurer said.

"Yeah, considering the way this turned out," I said and hung up.

We flew to McGrath in the morning. The snow was really deep—four to five feet on the level. We got over to Ace Airway. They said they'd try to get us in. We got some groceries to take out to the mine and stayed overnight in McGrath.

From the Ace Airway plane, I could make out the buildings at the camp and saw moose tracks in the snow. The pilot managed to land and agreed to return the day after tomorrow. I hoped there wouldn't be a blizzard.

The snow was deep, and it was tough going down the trail. The Arizona fellow was way behind. I slowed down and waited. When he got to me, he said, "I have to be pretty careful since I've got heart trouble. I don't know if I can carry my luggage down there."

This is no place for someone with heart trouble, I thought.

"Well, you could just take your sleeping bag," I said. "I've got my own stuff to carry."

I went on ahead and got a fire started in the cookhouse stove. The guy finally came in red-faced, dragging his luggage, huffing and puffing. I got worried then. I hoped he would come through this trip alive.

By then, the cookhouse was warm and cozy. The fellow got out his diagrams of the trommel he figured would save all this gold from the tailing piles. I knew it wouldn't work with the ground we had up here, but I kept my mouth shut.

When he opened his briefcase to show me the diagrams, I noticed it was half-full of magazines with girls on the covers. I thought that was strange baggage for a man with heart trouble to lug into a mining camp.

CHAPTER 20

Endings

In the morning, I went outside with the fellow from Arizona. The tailing piles were frozen solid. We chipped at them until the fellow collected enough material to fill a couple of canvas sacks the size of ten-pound sugar bags.

Then, he sat in the cookhouse, thawed it out, and panned. No gold. "Guess we'll have to go back out and chisel farther down in the piles," he said. We got a couple more sacks full, and he still didn't find any gold.

"If there was just some way I could take some gold back," the fellow said.

I studied the guy. "Well, if you just want gold from any old place, I can tell you where to get it. The mats from the bottom of the sluice box still have some gold in them from last fall. We can bring them in and shake them out on the floor."

He wanted to do that. So we brought the mats in, and he got all excited about gathering up an ounce and a half of gold off the floor. I watched him dump that gold into the sacks with the dirt from the tailings.

"Hey, why'd you do that?" I asked.

"Oh, I've got to show this to them when I get back," he said.

I left the room. I didn't have any stomach for this whole thing. I guess what you do is your business, buddy, I thought.

I was glad the weather cooperated so Ace Airway could pick us up without difficulty. I didn't relish the thought of being snowed-in out here with this character for company. When we got home, all of my attention went to the auction. As I worked on equipment, I hoped that luck would be with us the day of the sale. We'd need good weather and a big crowd of people in the mood to buy.

On March 25, I got a letter from White Wolf Mining saying there would be a meeting on April 10. All fourteen of the investors planned to be present. I thought about the guy from Arizona and wondered what would happen at the meeting.

Meanwhile, we got all of the machinery in good running condition and started moving it out to the field behind the hog barns. That's where we'd hold the auction.

The day of the auction, April 4, was sunny with a gentle south wind. My brother Ray came up from Two Harbors to be with me.

"Is there any way we could've worked it out to hold on to the place, Otis?" he asked.

I shook my head. "I don't think so, Ray," I said. "It wouldn't be worth it. Dave would be a slave to this place the rest of his life, and I'm too old to start farming again."

"At least you and Audrey have the house and a little land. And you've got your mine in Alaska."

"We do have the house and the land, but I'm not too sure about the mine, Ray," I said.

The sale started at eleven in the morning. People came pouring in. Some of them parked a mile and a half down the road and walked to the field when parking got tight. I started up each piece of equipment as it was being sold.

The funny thing was, the old hay balers and swathers and other old pieces of equipment did pretty well, but the newer equipment went for less than I'd hoped. For example, the tractor I paid thirty-five thousand dollars for a couple of years ago only brought sixteen thousand.

My kids—Dave, Randy, Terri, and Linda—were all there, looking pretty somber. I walked by Randy's pickup and saw he had bought our old log chain and some other stuff. Randy hadn't cared too much for farming, so I said, "I thought you got enough of that as a kid."

"Those things bring back memories of when we worked hard clearing fields on this place, Dad," Randy said. "I always had to fetch that chain to pull the tractor or Cat out when we got stuck. I figured I'd better save that old chain."

The Gemmell 4-H served hot dogs, hamburgers, coffee, and lemonade during the sale. Terri told me they made more than four hundred dollars.

"Maybe we should've served the lunch and given the machinery away," I joked, but my heart felt heavy.

Lots of people came up to me to shake my hand. That made me feel a little better. Toward the end of the sale, a neighbor to the west came over and sat down by me.

"Otis, I gave my whole life to my farm, and I should be doing what you are—getting out of farming. Land values keep dropping."

Another man stopped to say, "I've driven a truck by this place for twenty years, and watched it grow from brush and timber to a good-looking farm. Are you retiring, Otis?"

"Not exactly," I said. "My son took over the land, but the farm scene is bad."

He nodded. "I've seen farm auction after farm auction all over the country. But it must bother you to see your stuff auctioned off."

"Well, I've been worried about the farm for a couple of years. Sure, it's hard to have a sale like this, but in a way, it's kind of a relief. I don't need to worry about the farm any longer."

Audrey served a big roast beef dinner with mashed potatoes, gravy, and corn to all of our family at our house that night. We were a dispirited bunch, especially Dave. When we had a few minutes alone, I told him, "Dave, I know it's hard, but now you've got time to sell the land. The FHA will go along with you for a couple of years: they sure don't want the land back. They've got too much land on their hands. Just keep up the taxes on it and get on with the rest of your life."

The grandkids were running around. Shane started singing, and Terri said, "Shane, I think we've heard enough about Grandpa and the bear."

"Wait a minute," I said. "He's added something. Sing it again, Shane."

"Grandpa was there, and he shot a bear in his underwear," Shane sang.

"If you keep going, you'll have a whole song to sing," I said to young Shane. We grinned at each other.

On April 7, an investor called to see where I stood on having the books audited. "I'm absolutely going to push for that," I said. "If they don't want to do it, I'll hire someone to do it on my own."

He said, "There are a few of us that think it's a good idea, too."

"Well, then you fellows need to stand behind me on the tenth," I said.

The April 10 meeting included some investors I hadn't met before. The fellow from Arizona was there, too. He had his sacks and some magnifying glasses on the table. He was telling them how a trommel would be the thing to use on the tailing piles and the ground up there. A trommel is a long tubular device with a rounded, fitted punch plate. You put the material in one end, it rolls around in there, and the fine gold falls through the punch plate holes into a small sluice box under it.

I told the investors that a trommel could be used on the tailing piles but it wouldn't work on the virgin ground. "The pay is in the decomposed bedrock, a clayish-type of material.

In some cases, a trommel can be very successful, but it's not suited to certain types of ground."

I also told them the 50 percent gold loss they'd been quoted was a wild and inaccurate guess. In fact, the way I built and monitored the new sluice box reduced our loss to around 1 to 3 percent. But the Arizona fellow had the gold from the mats out on the table and was showing that to them. If they wanted to send that fellow up there, well, they would learn what I just told them the hard way.

"Otis, when do you think you should be up there this year?" one investor asked during the meeting.

I said, "My crew is ready. I'd like to be up on April 15."

There was a hush in the room. The chairman spoke up. "We don't think it's necessary for you to go until May 1."

"Then there might not be any mining this season," I said.

"Why? Would you explain that?" asked someone.

"We spent thousands of dollars putting in a big reservoir, gentlemen. It's important to be there in the spring when the water comes down from the high hills into the ditch that connects the reservoir to Cripple Creek. If the spillway gets clogged with debris, then we'll be likely to lose our reservoir. If you lose that, it'll take a year just to get things in order because the cut and drains will be clogged with gravel."

Another investor piped up, "Also, Otis, we think you shouldn't hire help down here and pay their expenses all the way up and back. You could hire help up there. You're paying your crew way too much. Last year, you paid your cook seventy-five dollars a day. I can go out on the street and hire a cook for forty dollars a day right here. And I know there are lots of heavy-equipment operators up in Alaska for hire."

I listened. In a way, it was a relief to have them get their cards out on the table.

I agreed that you could hire help up in Alaska, but that was risky. You don't know what kind of workers you're getting.

"Sir," I said to the investor who'd just talked, "are you speaking for yourself or the board? If you're speaking for the board, then I think you should make a motion that I do these things you want."

A motion was made and seconded about hiring workers in Alaska. My head was swimming. I stood up and excused myself, said I'd use the restroom and be right back.

I felt like I had been kicked in the stomach. I stood in there and took some deep breaths. What the investors were suggesting was unacceptable to me. I could not mine under the conditions they were proposing. And I was pretty sure that's exactly why those proposals were made: this was a sure way of getting rid of me.

The restroom door opened. One of the investors who'd been supportive in the past came in. "So what are you going to do, Otis?" he asked.

"It's pretty clear that I'll have to resign. If they're going to try to run the mine from down here, it'll never work. I put up with their indecisiveness for two years. Evidently, they're listening to that clown from Arizona. It'll cost seventy-five thousand to a hundred thousand dollars to get a trommel in there. We have a good set-up. I want no part of this."

The investor said, "I hate to see what's happening. I've got a feeling that it'll all fall apart in a couple of years."

"If you want to do something for me, you can go in with me and announce my resignation."

"Are you sure you want to do that?" he asked.

"As sure as I've ever been about anything in my life," I said.

We walked back into the room. The investors were clustered around the Arizona guy's gold pan.

The investor who walked in with me said, "I have good news for some of you and bad news for the rest of us. Otis has resigned."

I saw smiles on some faces and disappointment on others.

Then I told them the terms I had in mind—the escape plan I'd hit upon when I was fishing for grayling, in case the board refused to change the way the finances and communications were handled.

"I have a promissory note at the bank for twenty-eight thousand dollars to finance my share in White Wolf Mining. I expect you guys to pay it off. I want nothing more to do with this mining corporation. I also want a letter from you stating that I've always been honest and did a good job running the mine. I'm going to leave the room for awhile. When I come back, I want your decision on that."

My terms were agreed to. They said they'd send someone to pick up the van the next day. I told them I'd turn it over to them when they gave me payment for the note and the letter.

On the drive home, all by myself in the car, I fumed and swore. It helped ease the pain deep inside. At least, the way it worked out, I wouldn't have to put up with the whims of the board when it came to paying bills. I was glad to be done with that.

The lights were still on at midnight when I got home. Audrey was waiting for me. "Well, you don't need to worry about going back to Bear Creek," I told her. "I resigned."

Audrey fixed cups of hot chocolate, and I told her what happened. She listened quietly, then said, "It's the right decision, Otis. Can you imagine trying to work with the sort of crew you'd get hiring at the last minute out there?"

Sleep didn't come right away that night. I lay in bed thinking about the thrill of seeing gold in our sluice box and about that first night in the cookhouse with old Jim. I'd have to let him know that I wouldn't be back. And David Strant, too. And of course, my mining crew. I felt anger toward some of the White Wolf Mining board members, but most of all, I was very sad. God knows, I'd miss the mine and the Alaska Bush. The Bear Creek mine was my dream. It would be hard to let go.

The next day, Audrey wrote letters to David Strant and Jim for me, and I called the crew. Tim was shocked and disappointed. I told him to find a market for the ivory, and I'd contact a trucker hauling to Alaska who'd get the stuff out of there for us right away.

"Otis, Dingo's been gone all day yesterday and today," Audrey said on April 15. We went out looking for him but didn't have any luck. None of the neighbors had seen him. My Alaska Dingo dog had just plain disappeared. At dusk, I walked out in the yard and stared out over the fields. Dingo'd been with me the two seasons at the mine. Now I wouldn't be going back, and Dingo was gone. I stayed outside a long time, walking and thinking.

A few days later, my brother, Ray, called. "I heard you resigned from White Wolf Mining."

"That's right, Ray," I said.

"If you're looking for something to do, I've got a job to propose to you. I want to build a big reservoir on the creek in front of my cabin and put rainbow trout in there. Would you be interested in doing that this summer?"

"That sounds mighty tempting," I said.

"You can bring Audrey along and stay in the cabin."

"I'll talk it over with Audrey and call you back in an hour," I said.

Audrey didn't have a moment's hesitation. "That's just what we need. We'll get to enjoy ourselves a little bit, too."

That's how we ended up spending the summer. In early fall, I ran into Gene Bradley, the guy who took over as president of White Wolf Mining. He looked thin and tired.

He'd been out at the mine and called the summer "a disaster." The man from Arizona ran his trommel for two hundred hours and only recovered nineteen ounces of gold. The cook they hired quit. Their heavy equipment operators got the big tractor stuck and couldn't get it out for three weeks.

I listened and didn't say much. Before we parted, I asked

Gene if he'd seen a couple of ravens hanging around the camp.

"As a matter of fact, Otis, I did. Why do you ask?"

"Oh, I just wondered if that pair was still around."

All that summer, I'd thought about the mine. The guy who warned me about mining corporations sure turned out to be right. And I wondered what had happened to our Dingo dog. Audrey and I talked about him. I told her he probably got in some farmer's pasture and chased cows and got shot. Or maybe a game warden shot him for chasing deer.

There was another possibility, one that I liked better than the others. "You know, Audrey, it's sixty-five miles to the Canadian border straight north through the woods," I told her one night when we were sitting on the porch at Ray's cabin listening to the crickets. "Maybe Dingo just took off and he's out there in the woods—catching rabbits and chasing moose."

Audrey reached over and squeezed my hand. "Maybe that Dingo dog is just living wild out in the woods, Otis. Maybe he is."

I leaned back in my porch chair and studied the pale yellow moon shining above the spruce trees. In my mind, I pictured Dingo bounding after a rabbit in a meadow in the northern woods, back in the wilderness and living free.

Epilogue

Audrey and I still live in the little yellow house on the old home place in Mizpah, Minnesota. I raise raspberries and strawberries and do a lot of fishing. We've been lucky. We've been married forty-six years and have four healthy children and six grandchildren.

Back in 1984, after I built the reservoir for Ray at his cabin, I heard that a fellow I know was superintendent for a construction outfit out of California and Wyoming. I gave him a call.

"Get yourself out here, Otis," he said. "I've got all kinds of work for you. Right now, I've got a big loader coming in and you can drive that."

So Audrey and I went to Wyoming, and I worked out there awhile. Later, I worked for Ray's company traveling around through Canada and down in the Carolinas, demonstrating the machine Ray manufactures. Some time later, we went back to Alaska and tried prospecting for gold and helped friends of ours run a motel in the Yukon near Kluane Park—but that's another story. Now Audrey's taken a position at the center for handicapped people back in Northome.

The last I heard, White Wolf Mining was pretty much at a standstill, all the equipment sitting up there unused. Given the turn of events, I feel lucky to have gotten out when I did with reimbursement for my initial investment. I figure that placer mining will become a thing of the past, what with new environmental rules and regulations. But I'm glad I got my chance at mining gold in the Alaska Bush.

I still spend lots of time outdoors and often go to the Little Fork River in Minnesota. Not long ago, I headed up the river in my boat, rounded a bend, and saw a pair of shiny black ravens perched on a dead elm tree. That took me back to the night old Polly in Takotna village told me the mine was hexed. I wonder if the ravens are still hanging around the mine at Bear Creek.

Charlie's Gold and Other Frontier Tales
Kamron's first collection of short stories gives you adventure tales about men and women of the west, made up of cowboys, Indians, and settlers.
Written by Kent Kamron. (174 pgs.)
$15.95 each in a 6x9" paperback.
(plus $3.50 shipping & handling)

A Time For Justice
This second collection of Kamron's short stories takes off where the first volume left off, satisfying the reader's hunger for more tales of the wide praire.
Written by Kent Kamron. (182 pgs.)
$16.95 each in a 6x9" paperback.
(plus $3.50 shipping & handling)

Bonanza Belle
In 1908, Carrie Amundson left her home to become employed on a bonanza farm. One tragedy after the other befell her and altered her life considerably and she found herself back on the farm.
Written by Elaine Ulness Swenson. (344 pgs.)
$15.95 each in a 6x8-1/4" paperback.
(plus $3.50 ea. shipping & handling)

First The Dream
This story spans ninety years of Anna's life. She finds love, loses it, and finds in once again. A secret that Anna has kept is fully revealed at the end of her life.
Written by Elaine Ulness Swenson. (326 pgs.)
$15.95 each in a 6x8-1/4" paperback.
(plus $3.50 ea. shipping & handling)

Pete's New Family
Pete's New Family is a tale for children (ages 4-8) lovingly written to help youngsters understand events of divorce that they are powerless to change.
Written by Brenda Jacobson.
$9.95 each in a 5-1/2x8-1/2" paperback.
(plus $2.50 each shipping & handling) (price breaks after qty. of 10)

Country-fied

Stories with a sense of humor and love for country and small town people who, like the author, grew up country-fied . . . Country-fied people grow up with a unique awareness of their dependence on the land. They live their lives with dignity, hard work, determination and the ability to laugh at themselves.
Written by Elaine Babcock. (184 pgs.)
$14.95 each in a 6x9" paperback.
(plus $3.50 in shipping & handling)

COMING NOVEMBER 1st . . .

It Really Happened Here!

Relive the days of farm-to-farm salesmen and hucksters, of ghost ships and locust plagues when you read Ethelyn Pearson's collection of strange but true tales. It captures the spirit of our ancestors in short, easy to read, colorful accounts that will have you yearning for more.
Written by Ethelyn Pearson. (160 plus pgs.)
$24.95 each in an 8-1/2x11" paperback.
(plus $3.50 in shipping & handling)

Dr. Val Farmer's
Honey, I Shrunk The Farm

The first volume in a three part series on Rural Life is a frank look at the common toils of farming. The following issues are discussed in seven chapters: Farm Economics; Understanding The Farm Crisis; How To Cope With Hard Times; Families Going Through It Together; Dealing With Debt; Going For Help, Helping Others and Transitions Out of Farming.
Written by Val Farmer. (208 pgs.)
$16.95 each in a 6x9" paperback.
(plus $3.50 in shipping & handling)